DISCARD

P9-BBQ-492

EMMA'S
RIVER

Ω

Published by
PEACHTREE PUBLISHERS
1700 Chattahoochee Avenue
Atlanta, Georgia 30318-2112

www.peachtree-online.com

Text © 2010 by Alison Hart
Illustration © 2010 by Paul Bachem

All rights reserved. No part of this publication may be reproduced, stored in a retrieval
system, or transmitted in any form or by any means—electronic, mechanical, photocopy,
recording, or any other—except for brief quotations in printed reviews, without the prior
permission of the publisher.

Cover design by Loraine Joyner
Book design by Melanie McMahon Ives

Manufactured in December 2009 by RRD Donnelley South China in Guangdong
Province, China
10 9 8 7 6 5 4 3 2 1
First Edition

Library of Congress Cataloging-in-Publication Data
Hart, Alison, 1950-
  Emma's river / written by Alison Hart.
     p. cm.
  Summary: In 1852, Emma, her pregnant mother and her pony board the steamboat *Sally
May* to meet her father in St. Joseph, Missouri, but when the ship suddenly explodes in a
fiery blaze, Emma and all onboard must fight for their survival in the icy waters of the
Missouri River.
  ISBN 978-1-56145-524-9 / 1-56145-524-5
  [1. Steamboats--Fiction. 2. Voyages and travels--Fiction. 3. Disasters--Fiction. 4. Fires--
Fiction. 5. Survival--Fiction. 6. Missouri--History--19th century--Fiction.] I. Title.
  PZ7.H256272Em 2010
  [Fic]--dc22

                              2009024506

CIP
AC

EMMA'S RIVER

Alison Hart

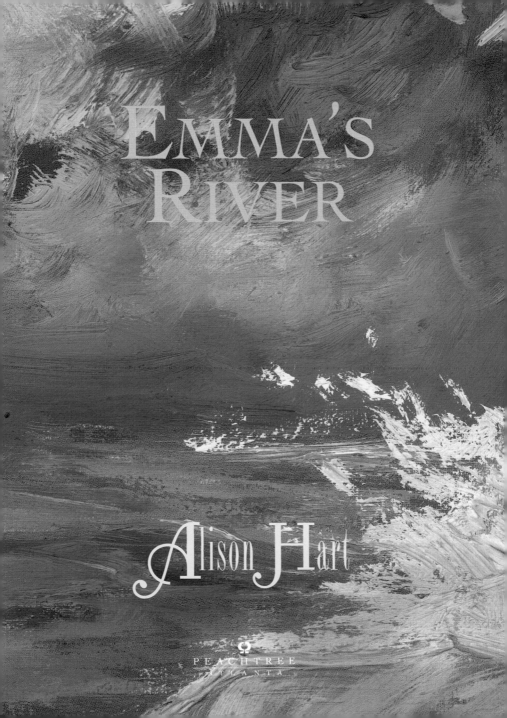

PEACHTREE
ATLANTA

To Captain Alan Bates
and his real steamboat stories
—A. H.

TABLE OF CONTENTS

Chapter One

April 1852

O uch, Mama, you're hurting me!" Emma Wright said crossly.

Mama's gloved hand tightened around her daughter's fingers. "We must hurry, Emma," she said. "Captain Digby said the *Sally May* leaves promptly at noon."

Mama tugged Emma around the carriages and wagons crowding the St. Louis wharf. A baggage van carrying their luggage and goods rumbled behind them. A Negro wearing a raggedy shirt strained as he pulled the heavy load.

Emma looked over her shoulder. Licorice Twist, her black pony, was tied to the cart. His shiny mane bounced with each quick step. Soon Mama, Emma, and Twist would be boarding the steamboat *Sally May*. They would travel up the Mississippi to the Missouri

River, which would take them to Kansas City. There they would meet Papa and travel together to St. Joseph. Then they would go west to California. Emma could barely wait. She missed her dear father, who had been gone too long.

For weeks Mama and the servants had sorted their belongings, packing only what they would need for the journey. Mama had agonized over every picture frame and teacup. Some furniture had been shipped ahead. Most had been left behind. Emma chose only the essentials for life in the Wild West: her boots, her riding habit, her pony.

"No, Emma, Twist must stay in St. Louis," Mama had said, her voice pinched. "One stubborn charge will be trouble enough on this journey."

But Emma had been determined. For four days, she pushed her plate away at mealtimes, leaving her food untouched.

Mama raised her eyes to the heavens.

For three days, Emma refused to speak.

Mama sipped Doctor John's Sarsaparilla Tonic.

On the last day, Emma held her breath. Her eyes bulged and her cheeks grew purple.

Mama took to her bed.

Emma placed a cold cloth on her mother's forehead and whispered, "Please, Mama."

With a deep sigh, Mama gave in. Emma had already packed Twist's brush and bucket.

Mama stopped on the wharf, out of breath. "Oh, where could Doctor Burton be?" she fussed.

Roustabouts, the men who loaded the cargo, swarmed around them. They pushed and pulled bales, barrels, and boxes. When they passed Emma, she crinkled her nose at their sweaty odor.

"Missus Wright!" A heavyset man wearing a wool waistcoat, silk hat, kid gloves, and patent leather boots strode toward them. Mama called him a doctor. Emma called him a dandy.

Mama waved. Her face was splotchy and she dabbed her cheeks with her handkerchief. "Doctor Burton! I was afraid you had forsaken us."

"Never in a thousand years." Tipping his hat, Doctor Burton bowed slightly. "Your husband entrusted me with your care on this trip. I aim to fulfill my duty."

Emma slipped to the back of the baggage van to check on Twist. The pony nuzzled her, hoping for a sweet. She pulled a sugar cube from the pocket of her pinafore. While the pony crunched his treat, Emma stood on tiptoe, glimpsing the tops of the steamboats. Dozens of the large paddlewheelers lined the wharf, their chimneys jutting into the hazy sky.

"Look, Twist," she told the pony excitedly. "The

Mississippi River! Soon we'll board the *Sally May*. You'll have a big stall filled with fresh hay and water. Mama says in ten days we'll be with Papa. Then we'll travel west to find gold."

"Emma!" Doctor Burton pointed his silver-handled cane at her. "Leave the beast and come with us. There's no time to dawdle."

Emma scowled. *Beast?* Twist was the most beautiful pony with the smoothest gaits in all of St. Louis!

"Twist will be fine, sweetheart." Mama's eyes smiled under her plumed hat. "Doctor Burton will see that your pony is brought aboard."

Emma glared doubtfully at the doctor. A bell rang.

"That is our signal to board," Doctor Burton said. "Come, ladies." Turning, he escorted Mama toward the steamboat, parting the scurrying roustabouts with swipes of his cane.

"You are not a *beast*." Emma gave her pony's silky neck a pat. "You are my dear friend."

"Look, Emma!" Mama waved at her to hurry. "There she is." The *Sally May* rose from the Mississippi, as tall as a three-story building. The steamboat was white, with gold and black trim. Pendants and flags snapped in the breeze. Its name was written in red scroll on the paddlewheel housing.

Hand on her hat, Emma tipped back her head so she could see the top of the two chimneys. They belched thick smoke. Above the pilothouse, gulls dove and soared. Emma's heart soared with them.

"Now I see why Captain Digby calls his steamboat a giant wedding cake," she said. Captain Digby, an old friend of her father's, had often dazzled the family with tales of river travel.

"And did he also call it a floating coffin?" Doctor Burton asked. "Why, just last month, the *Caddo* sank. Five dead. And the *May Queen* burst into flames—"

"Oh!" Mama slumped against the doctor.

Worried, Emma wrapped her arm around her mother's bustle.

"I am so sorry, Missus Wright," Doctor Burton said. Holding her up with one hand, he fanned her with the other. "I should not have spoken of such horrors in front of a lady in your condition."

Emma had no idea what Mama's condition was. But she had noticed lately that it required smelling salts and billowy dresses.

"Thank you," Mama said, righting herself. "These silly fainting spells last only moments."

"Emma, take charge of your mother while I commandeer the roustabouts. They need to load your luggage."

"Don't forget my pony, sir." Emma kept her arm around Mama. Doctor Burton hustled off, yelling orders and offering coins. Instantly the roustabouts surged toward the baggage van, grabbing valises, boxes, and trunks.

Emma watched as the men ran their goods on board the *Sally May*. On a second gangplank, other workers were loading mules and oxen.

"Git 'em loaded, yer jackdogs!" the first mate in charge bellowed as he hit a roustabout's shoulder with a sturdy stick. "Faster, faster, yer slimy snails!"

Minutes later, the first mate untied Twist from the cart. "Take good care of him, sir!" Emma called. But as he led the pony toward the line of oxen, he raised his stick as if to strike. Emma's jaw dropped. She ran over and planted herself in front of the first mate.

"Sir, that's *my* pony. He is *not* livestock that can be mercilessly beaten onto the boat!"

"Aye aye, m'lady." The mate saluted, his smile mocking her. Then he turned and growled, "Git up, yer long-eared mule." Using the end of the rope, he whacked Twist on the rump.

Emma grabbed the rope, furious at his rudeness. "I insist you treat my pony with kindness!"

The doctor bustled over. "Emma, let the man do his—"

"Doctor Burton," Mama cut in, her tone steely. "Pay the man to load my daughter's pony with care."

Doctor Burton blew out a frustrated breath. The mate held out a grimy palm. The doctor placed a coin in it. Reluctantly, Emma let go of the rope.

"All who's going to St. Joe get aboard!" the ship's clerk called.

"No more time to waste," Doctor Burton said. Grasping Emma's and Mama's elbows, he hurried them across the passengers' gangplank. When Emma jumped onto the deck, she looked back at Twist.

The first mate was yanking the pony across the other gangplank. "Git up now, yer stubb'rn donkey of the royal family."

Emma stamped her foot. *That wretched man!*

Suddenly Twist bolted forward, knocking into the mate. The man flew off the gangplank and landed in the river with a splash. The pony leaped nimbly on deck while the mate thrashed about in the shallow water, yelping in rage. Emma hid a giggle as the roustabouts pulled the cursing man onto the wharf.

The *Sally May*'s whistle sounded as the last of the passengers scurried across the gangplank. Women carried hatboxes and parasols. Men consulted watches and tickets. A family wearing homespun carried bundles on their heads. Other passengers hung over the low railing, bidding farewell in many languages. *"Auf Wiedersehen! Au revoir!* Good-bye!" rang through the air.

Emma looked over the railing, too. Below her, the muddy Mississippi swirled like spilled coffee.

"Haul it, yer slimy frogs!" The dripping-wet first mate struck right and left with his stick, taking out his embarrassment on the deckhands. They heaved the gangplank onto the bow. Steam rose from the chimneys with a piercing hiss. The paddlewheels turned with a *thunk, thunk.*

Goosebumps prickled up Emma's arms as the *Sally May* backed away from the St. Louis wharf. The mighty river was taking her, Mama, and Twist to Papa, the West, and adventure!

CHAPTER TWO

Quit dillydallying, Miss Emma," Doctor Burton's sharp voice cut into her thoughts. "We must get your mother away from this riffraff and into her stateroom."

Doctor Burton speared his cane into the crowd to part the milling passengers. Emma lurched after him, pretending that she didn't have her "sea legs" yet. She'd read about sea legs in the ocean tales section of one of her favorite books—*My Boys' and Girls' Magazine and Fireside Companion*. There weren't any waves big enough to rock the boat, but she was enjoying herself, weaving back and forth.

She pitched into a lady carrying two baskets and a crying baby. A toddler clung to the woman's grimy skirt. The little boy had dirty cheeks, and the baby's legs were scabby.

"Pardon me," Emma said, edging past them. A deck-hand holding a coiled line bumped her. She toppled against a barrel, snagging her stocking. Emma bent to inspect the rip, and someone rapped her on the shoulder with the tip of an umbrella. "Move, miss," a high-pitched voice ordered. When Emma straightened up, she was face-to-face with a small lady clutching a fuzzy white poodle. As the woman waltzed past, her wide skirts filled the pathway.

"Emma!" her mother called from a broad staircase. She was gripping Doctor Burton's elbow with one hand and pressing her handkerchief to her nose with the other. "Hurry, darling."

Emma sprinted for the stairway. She followed the doctor's coattails up the steps that led to the cabin circle. Passengers milled around the clerk's counter, waiting to register. Doctor Burton pushed to the front. When he came back he held up two keys. "This way." He nodded toward a set of double doors.

They walked through the doors into the steamboat's main cabin, a large room stuffed with ladies, gentlemen, and servants. Later, the main cabin would be used for dining and dancing. Now passengers scurried to and fro, trying to locate lost children, baggage, and staterooms.

"Your room is aft, toward the stern. That's the back of the steamboat," Doctor Burton explained to Emma.

She wanted to retort that Captain Digby had already taught her the correct terms. Instead she quipped, "And are the gentlemen's staterooms located *fore* toward the *bow?*"

Doctor Burton gave her an annoyed frown. Mama often scolded Emma for speaking her mind. *Children should be seen and not heard*, she always said. But Emma had no patience with sayings like that.

The doctor halted in front of a girl in a gray dress and starched white apron waiting in an open doorway. Her auburn hair was coiled in a knot and covered with a cloth cap. "Good day, Missus Wright. Miss Wright." She spoke in an Irish brogue like Mrs. McEnery, the kitchen cook they'd left behind in St. Louis. "Me name is Kathleen." The girl curtsied. "I'm at yer service."

"Missus Wright requires hot tea and a cool compress," Doctor Burton instructed. "Your mistress is in a delicate condition. You are to be at her service around the clock."

Kathleen curtsied again, her eyes downcast. Gently she grasped Mama's elbow to help her into the stateroom. Emma thought the new maid looked about sixteen, her cousin Minna's age. They'd left Minna and her family behind in St. Louis, too.

Emma stepped inside. The stateroom was half the size of her bedroom at home. Light shone through glass panes in the exterior door. It led to the veranda, the walkway that circled the outside of the steamboat. A double-bed berth with a single over it took up the right side of the room. A stand with pitcher and washbowl were tucked in an alcove. Underneath the stand sat a chamber pot. On the other side of the room was a small closet with hooks for their clothes.

"I'll wait here with you until your baggage is brought up," Doctor Burton said to Mama, who sank wearily onto the bottom berth. Kathleen began unpinning her mother's plumed hat.

Emma fidgeted, wanting to explore the steamboat and find Twist.

Even after Kathleen got Mama settled with tea, they waited. Outside the doorway, Doctor Burton passed the time chatting with other gentlemen. Finally a red-faced porter dragged a trunk into the room. A second porter staggered in behind him carrying a valise, some bags, and Emma's smaller trunk. Doctor Burton bid them good day and turned to leave.

"I'm coming with you," Emma said. "I must check on my pony."

"You will not do any such thing." Doctor Burton bent so close that his nose bumped her hat brim. "You are forbidden to go below. Your pony, Twitch—"

"*Twist,*" Emma corrected him. "As in *licorice twist.*"

"Whatever its name is, the animal will be well cared for. I'll make sure of it. The main deck is too dangerous for a scatterbrained child. Do you understand?"

Scatterbrained child! Emma bristled. *This man is not Papa, and I will* not *obey him*, she decided. She stood her ground and glared at Doctor Burton.

"I hope that is clear." The doctor straightened and turned to Mrs. Wright. "Your daughter will be safe with me," he told her. "You must rest."

"Thank you, Doctor Burton." Mama fell back on the bed with a sigh. "Mind your manners, Emma," she called as Kathleen began unlacing her boots. "And obey Doctor Burton."

Muttering "I surely will not" to herself, Emma marched after the doctor. By now, most of the passengers had found their staterooms. Still, the gentlemen's end of the main cabin was packed. A group of men stood by a bar. They were laughing and spitting tobacco juice into a brass spittoon, which stood on the floor like a plant pot. Other men huddled around tables, playing cards. Cabin boys bustled past, serving drinks from trays. Cigar smoke clouded the air.

Doctor Burton joined one of the tables of card players. Emma watched as he fanned the cards he'd been

dealt. Around him, the other players tossed coins in the middle. One man spit a wad of chewing tobacco onto the wood floor. Another plopped his feet onto the seat beside him as he studied his hand.

"Emma, join the other children in the ladies' end of the parlor," the doctor said.

"Sir, I'm not a child," Emma protested. "I'm almost eleven."

Doctor Burton gestured to a thin young man, who hurried over. His brown hair was parted in the middle and slicked back with perfumed oil. He wore a starched white shirt with a nameplate identifying him as Arthur Jenkins, Third Clerk.

"Mister Jenkins, see to it that Miss Emma finds company her own age," Doctor Burton said, his gaze on his cards.

"Yes, sir," Mister Jenkins replied.

"And make sure she does *not* go below," Doctor Burton added. To Emma, he said, "Mind the mud clerk, now. I'll find you in time for supper."

The mud clerk. Emma knew that was one of the lowliest workers on the ship. Even less chance she was going to mind him!

"Come, miss. Rules must be obeyed." Mister Jenkins nodded toward the wall. Signs dotted the red plush wallpaper: Gambling Strictly Forbidden. No Spitting. Boots off the Furniture. "I'm sure you'll find someone playing Tiddlywinks or Old Maid in the ladies' parlor," he added, pointing in the other direction. Then, opening a door marked "Clerk's Office," he left her.

Old Maid! With a humph, Emma clomped from the gentlemen's area. *If only Papa were here. He'd take me to see Twist.*

She crossed the midship gangway, a passage with doors at the end that led to the outside of the steamboat. A rainbow of dancing lights caught her attention. Above, the sun glimmered through skylights made of colored glass. Crystal chandeliers reflected the colorful beams, turning the area into a twinkling fairyland. Emma twirled a few times, pretending she was waltzing with Papa.

Whack! "Ouch!" Emma clapped a palm to her stinging ear and glared into the narrowed eyes of the lady with the umbrella.

"Watch where you're going, you muddleheaded girl!" the woman said. The poodle, still clutched in her arms, bared its needle teeth.

Emma backed away quickly, rubbing her ear.

The ladies' end of the steamboat cabin was carpeted. Emma looked around, marveling at the brocade-covered sofas, candelabras, gilded mirrors, and a potbellied stove surrounded by rocking chairs. Smartly dressed matrons and fashionable girls gossiped, embroidered, played piano, and read Bibles. Chambermaids served tea and crumpets.

Emma grabbed a crumpet from a lowered tray. She settled onto a rocker, swaying to and fro as she chewed the powdery sweet. "Did you glimpse the heavenly blue of Professor Almond's eyes?" one young lady said. "Why, he's a poem!"

"And did you hear the gentleman who spoke with a British accent?" the other young woman fluttered. "His servant addressed him as *Lord* Highbatten. I was smitten!" With that, the two broke into a fit of giggling.

Emma rolled her eyes. As far as she could see, there was not a whit of adventure in the ladies' parlor.

Stuffing the last of the crumpet into her mouth, she bolted for a door at the end of the parlor. *Dash the rules.* She was going to find Twist.

She swung open the door, only to find the ladies' retiring room. Sachets of rose petals dotted the washbowl stand and the toilet, a hole in a wooden seat. Holding her nose, Emma peered curiously into the hole. River water flashed far beneath. *Pee-ew.*

Emma quickly shut the door and hurried back to the midship gangway. She really needed to find Twist. For all she knew, the first mate had treated her pony as roughly as he'd treated the roustabouts.

She turned to go to the larboard, the left side, of the steamboat. Once outside, she peered over the veranda railing and watched the Mississippi flow past like melted chocolate. In the distance, she could see St. Louis. The late afternoon sun shone on the roofs of the town's shops. A pang filled her. Would she ever see her home again?

No. The river was taking her to a new home—and to Papa.

The sun was sinking and the afternoon was waning. Soon it would be supper time and Doctor Burton would come searching for her. She had to hurry.

Couples strolled along the veranda. "Pardon me, pardon me," Emma said as she bustled past them to the main stairway.

Hesitating on the top step, she stared down to the main deck. Squeals, cries, bellows, hisses, and clangs rose from below. A deckhand was tying a line. Another worker rolled a barrel closer to the wall and secured it in place. The smell of burning wood, rotting fruit, and sweating animals wafted upward.

You are forbidden to go below. It is too dangerous...

Emma was no stranger to rules. *Speak in turn. Walk*

with small gliding steps. Take dainty bites. And she had broken many of them. But her disobedience had never put her in danger. *Maybe I should go back to our stateroom and look for Twist later,* she thought.

Then she pictured her beloved Twist among the oxen and hogs. Taking a deep breath, Emma started down the stairs. Step by hesitant step, she made her way to the forbidden main deck.

CHAPTER THREE

Fingers grasped Emma's upper arm, yanking her backward. "Oh!" She caught herself on the railing before she fell.

"Halt this instant, Miss Wright." On the top step, Arthur Jenkins, the mud clerk, stared down at her, his arms folded across his chest.

"How dare you grab me!" she retorted.

"How dare *you* disobey Doctor Burton's orders!" The toe of his leather shoe tapped the wooden step.

"What are the doctor's orders to you?"

"He paid me handsomely to keep you out of trouble." Putting one hand in his pocket, he jingled several coins.

"He paid *you* to keep me out of trouble so *he* can smoke and gamble? How clever of him." Turning, Emma stomped back up the stairs. She didn't know who she was more vexed at, the meddling mud clerk or the sneaky doctor. Then an idea came to her. "Mister

Jenkins. You are the clerk in charge of baggage, are you not?" she asked.

"I am." He tilted his nose in the air.

"Then I have some valuable baggage for you to check on. My pony Licorice—"

His mouth flew open. "Caring for livestock is not my responsibility."

"My pony is *not* livestock. He is my dear friend."

Mister Jenkins smirked. "Then perhaps you should have bought him a ticket for cabin passage."

"Oh, you are so rude." Emma tossed her brown curls. Pushing past him, she strode down the veranda. The clerk followed behind. "You do not need to escort me," she told him.

"Alas, miss, I do."

"I am only going to my stateroom."

"Which is on the starboard side. And you are marching around the larboard side."

Emma stopped, realizing she'd gotten herself all tangled up. But she wasn't going to admit it to the lowly clerk. "Fine, then. I was really going above to see Captain Digby." She gave Mister Jenkins a winning smile, like the one Cousin Minna used when she wanted to get her way. "Did you know that the captain and I are friends?" She stared with pretend anger at her upper arm. Her dress sleeve was wrinkled where he'd grasped it. "Perhaps I should mention to him how one of his employees *mistreated* a valued passenger."

Mister Jenkin's brows shot up and sweat beaded on his skinny moustache.

"But no. I'm quite sure you were only doing your job." Again, Emma beamed at him. "Rest assured, I will put in a good word for you. However, then you might owe me a favor?"

He swiped the sweat off his upper lip. "I believe *not* telling Doctor Burton what his silly charge was up to is favor enough."

"Fiddlesticks." Emma stamped her foot before marching off again. Mister Jenkins followed her until she reached the narrow stairway leading up to the hurricane deck. By then, she'd decided she really did want to see Captain Digby. Perhaps if she pleaded, *he* would take her below to check on Twist. Or at least give her permission to go. If not, the pilothouse was sure to be more exciting than the ladies' parlor.

"Supper is in thirty minutes." Jenkins consulted his pocket watch. "Ladies and *children*," he said, "and their male escorts dine first. Doctor Burton expects you to be prompt."

"Obviously his appetite is more important to him

than my pony," Emma grumbled. Without so much as a good day to the clerk, she turned away and climbed the narrow stairs. When her head poked into the evening light, she gasped in delight at the rush of the wind and the closeness of the clouds.

Above her, dark smoke streamed from the tall chimneys. Cinders pattered like rain onto the deck, which was covered with sand so it wouldn't catch fire. Since supper would soon be served, there were few strollers on this level.

A railing circled the deck. Emma hurried past a red fire barrel brimming with water and a wooden rack filled with empty buckets. She pressed against the railing, the wind tugging at her hat ribbons. Far below her the Mississippi writhed like a brown snake. Cottonwood trees lined the banks. A flock of black-necked geese lifted off from a sandbar.

"Miss Emma Wright!"

She spun toward the familiar voice. Captain Digby, dressed in his trim black suit, waved. Tall and stately, he stood on the stairs leading to the Texas deck, the smaller one that held the captain's and officers' rooms. Perched behind him on top of the Texas, like the uppermost tier of a wedding cake, was the pilothouse.

He waved again, this time signaling her to join him. Emma ran across the deck.

"I feel as if I could touch the sky!" she declared when she reached him.

"Well, the pilothouse *is* sixty feet above the river," he said. Then he frowned, looking like Papa when he was displeased. "Why in all nation are you running around the ship unescorted, Miss Emma?"

"Mama is resting, Doctor Burton is gambling, and Mister Jenkins is cataloging mud," she recited.

Captain Digby laughed. "Fortunate that you found your way up here. You'll be safe under my watch." He pointed to the pilothouse. "Come, there are a few moments left before supper. I'll show you how to navigate my steamboat."

Emma clapped her hands. At last, an adventure!

"This way, m'lady." He swept his arm toward the stairs, beckoning her to go up and enter the pilothouse. Breathless with anticipation, Emma climbed to the top. A man with his back to her stood on one side of a great spoked steering wheel almost as tall as he was. She could only see half of the wheel. The rest of it disappeared into a slot in the floor. Brass knobbed ropes hung from the roof on both sides. The floor was covered with oilcloth. Along the back wall were an unlit stove and a bench, for visitors, she supposed.

Captain Digby introduced the man at the wheel. "Miss Emma, this is our pilot, Mister LaBarge. He's in charge of steering the *Sally May* up the Missouri."

Emma blinked in amazement. The pilot wore a cap of striped fur, an animal's black nose poking from the fuzzy crown. His face was bronzed by the sun and deep lines cut across his forehead. A whittled toothpick jutted from beneath a bushy mustache, which bristled as if alive.

Mister LaBarge winked at Emma. "I might not be the captain of this leaky vessel," he said, the toothpick bobbing up and down. "But I am personally acquainted with every bar, snag, landing, and woodyard along the Mississippi and Missouri."

"A boastful statement if I ever heard one," Captain Digby told Emma with a wink of his own. "But Mister LaBarge *is* a lightning pilot."

"Aye, I can read these rivers like a schoolgirl reads a primer."

"*Read* a river?" Emma repeated.

"Look here. I'll show you." The pilot waved her closer. Emma stepped next to him. If she stood on tiptoe, she could see out the open front of the pilothouse. The sun was slowly setting, turning the river into a golden-red ribbon.

Mister LaBarge pointed ahead. "See those ripples in the water to yer left?" She nodded. "See how they slant? That tells me 'gravel reef ahead.' If we hit that reef, the *Sally May* could stop dead in the river."

"We don't want that."

"Nay, we do not. Traveling upstream, the *Sally May*'s slow enough." He pointed to the right. "See that circular whirl? That signals a snag."

"A snag is a tree that's fallen into the river," Captain Digby explained. "If the *Sally May* is unlucky enough to ram a big one, it could split her hull and we'd sink."

Emma gasped. "Sink? Just like that?"

"Aye." Mister LaBarge pointed straight ahead. "See that rough water stretching bank to bank?"

"Another gravel reef? We mustn't hit it!"

Captain Digby chuckled. "No, it's a false reef, made by the wind."

"Fiddlesticks." Emma frowned. "I'll never get the hang of reading the river."

"Don't be impatient, young lady. It takes hundreds of trips up and down these waters to master them," Mister LaBarge said.

As Emma looked ahead, the sun disappeared behind a grove of cottonwoods. The air grew cooler and shifting shadows blackened the river. She watched carefully, wanting to "read" the river, too. But in the fading light she could barely tell land from water. "How do you steer in the dark, Mister LaBarge?"

With a solemn look, he tapped his chest. "A good pilot knows the shape of the river—every channel and bend—deep in his heart."

She reached high up for a rope hanging nearby. "May I—?"

"No, Emma!" Captain Digby thundered behind her. She snatched back her hand. "Ring the bell," he said, "and you may cause a riot below."

"Oh!" Emma was glad she hadn't caused a riot.

"The bells are used to signal the engineers to stop, go ahead, back up, or proceed full steam ahead," he explained. "Can you imagine the confusion?"

"Sorry, sir," Emma said. "I didn't mean any harm."

"Apology accepted. You cannot ring the bell, but here, place your hands on the pilotwheel."

Emma gripped the handles. The curved top of the wheel rose high to her left. Beneath her fingertips, she could feel the power of the mighty river.

"See? You are steering the *Sally May*."

Emma spied a faint light swinging to and fro before the bow. Squinting, she tried to see what it was.

"Raft ahead!" Mister LaBarge suddenly shouted.

Emma's heart flew into her throat. The light was growing closer. If that *was* a raft, the *Sally May* would smash it to pieces!

CHAPTER FOUR

Mister LaBarge seized the wheel on the left side, spinning it down so quickly that it tore from Emma's grasp. Losing her balance, she tumbled to the floor. At the same time, he yanked the bell ropes, setting off a loud clanging below.

"Raft dead ahead!" the pilot shouted into a speaking tube. "Ease up! Ease up!"

The steamboat slowly veered starboard. From the raft, an angry voice shouted, "Watch where yer goin', yer hog-carryin' scow!"

Captain Digby helped Emma to her feet. Stepping back, he lit his pipe. Emma righted her hat and stood on tiptoe again. She placed her hands gently on the pilotwheel handles, but let Mister LaBarge do the steering.

The raft floated safely past, the voices of its occupants soon distant. Hurrahs and cheers rose from the main deck of the *Sally May*.

"You did it, Mister LaBarge!" Emma said.

"Blasted raft should've had a bigger signal light." He grinned as he spoke, the waxed ends of his mustache curving downward.

"That was very exciting," Emma said. "It was almost a disaster."

"For the raft, perhaps," Captain Digby said. "But the *Sally May* is a floating fortress and Mister LaBarge its able commander. No raftman's pile of logs will keep us from reaching St. Joe."

"I believe it," Emma said.

Mister LaBarge smoothly steered the *Sally May* back on course. Once again, the pilothouse hummed with the patter of the paddlewheels and the pilot's low singing. Holding tightly to the wheel handles, Emma gazed ahead. The sky was silver, the water black. She could feel the lure of the river, and she grinned as wide as Mister LaBarge.

Then shouts of the workers rising from the main deck reminded her of her earlier quest. "Captain Digby, my pony Licorice Twist is penned below on the main deck. I would like to check on him—"

"Below?" The captain nearly dropped his pipe. Yanking the end from his mouth, he pointed it at her. "Proper young ladies do *not* go below to the main deck. Your mother would be aghast."

"But I need to make sure that Twist is——"

"Do not fret, Miss Emma. I will personally check on your pony." He lowered his voice. "I wouldn't want you to end up like Harry Bixby."

"Harry Bixby?"

Captain Digby nodded. "On our last trip, Harry Bixby, a nosy little boy, had the misfortune to disobey rules and sneak down to the main deck."

"What happened?" Emma asked.

The pilot answered her this time. "Our mud clerk Mister Jenkins caught him."

"What did Mister Jenkins do?" Emma asked.

Mister LaBarge snorted. "Made *me* stop the boat so he could kick Harry off. Set him on shore—in the wilderness."

Emma gasped. "That's terrible!"

"Indeed it is." Mister LaBarge's mustache twitched. Was he laughing? Emma glanced at Captain Digby. His lips were clamped tightly to his pipe stem but his eyes danced.

Was the story of Harry Bixby true? Emma wasn't

sure. Grown-ups were always telling tales to make children behave. Didn't Mama point out—over and over—the lessons to be learned in *Aesop's Fables*? But she decided to be careful. It *could* have happened.

"A well-mannered girl like you has naught to worry about of course," Captain Digby added.

"I suppose," Emma said. "Will you check on Twist after supper, then? I won't be able to rest unless I know my pony has feed and water."

"Yes, yes, my dear. This evening," the captain said. But he sounded almost as impatient as Doctor Burton.

Emma sighed. Once again, she wished Papa was here. *He* would know how important Twist was to her.

"Now let's get to more tasty affairs." The captain held out his elbow. "Allow me to escort you to the main cabin and the delicious supper that awaits us. I hear the cook has prepared a bounty of dishes: squirrel pie, possum stew, and who knows what other delights."

"Thank you, Mister LaBarge, for a gripping adventure," Emma said politely to the pilot before leaving. Taking the captain's arm, she let him lead her from the pilothouse. But she wasn't thinking of squirrel pie or the near-accident. Her thoughts were on Twist.

As they entered the main cabin a few minutes later, she realized that Captain Digby had been talking to her.

"The *Sally May*," he was saying, "is a floating hotel for its distinguished guests. The crew leaves no wish unanswered, no desire unmet."

Emma was tempted to ask him, *why can't I see Twist, then?* But for once she held her tongue.

The gentlemen's end of the main cabin had been changed into a dining room. Waiters bustled to and fro carrying trays of steaming dishes, which they placed on a long table laid with silverware, pitchers, and plates. Most of the ladies and children were already seated. Doctor Burton hurried over as soon as he spied Emma.

"Allow me." He held out his own arm to her. "Captain Digby, are you in command of this table?"

"Indeed," the captain said. "Miss Emma, I leave you in the doctor's capable hands." Then he strode off to greet a group of passengers who were calling to him. Soon he was lost in the sea of diners, and Emma knew there was no use reminding him about Twist.

"Is Mama not eating?" Emma asked as Doctor Burton whisked her around the table to two empty places.

"She is still tired. Your servant girl will take a tray to her." He pulled out a chair. "Sit, child. We must eat before the table is empty of food."

Emma slid into the seat. She took off her hat and

placed it on her lap. In front of her, a mountain of cold meat rose from a platter. To her right and left were bowls heaped with food. If this was supper, the lightest meal of the day, she doubted the table would ever be empty.

"Emma, look lively." Doctor Burton thrust a tureen at her. Impatiently setting it down, he grabbed a platter and spooned a mound of spiced pigshead onto his plate.

Emma stared at the contents of the bowl beside her. Fish heads and tails floated in a murky sea of broth. She was still deciding whether she was brave enough to try it when the diner next to her snatched up the tureen.

"You, waiter! More bread!" Doctor Burton called. Cries for more soup, more pastries, more meat rose in the air. The room echoed with the clattering of forks and clinking of spoons.

Emma filled her own plate with cheese, nuts, fruits, and a roll. While she ate, she watched the other diners, who chomped and slurped as if their manners had been left ashore.

When she had eaten as much as she could, Emma dabbed her mouth with a napkin. "Doctor Burton, were you able to check on Twist today?" she asked.

"Of course," he replied, his gaze intent on a platter of turkey. "Your pony is fine."

"Thank you," Emma said. But as she watched Doctor Burton gnaw a drumstick, an unladylike thought came over her: the doctor was *not* telling the truth. Slowly, she picked up an almond. "And was his stall knee-deep with straw?" she asked. She popped the almond into her mouth, trying not to sound too curious.

He nodded as he tore off a chunk of meat with his teeth. "Soft as a feather bed."

"And his mane and tail white as snow and brushed until silky?"

"I brushed them myself."

Narrowing her eyes, Emma stared at the grease dripping from his chin. Doctor Burton was not telling the truth. Twist's mane and tail were coal black.

Angrily, she grabbed two apples from a fruit bowl and stuck them into the pocket of her pinafore. Then she dropped her napkin on the table and stood. She could spin her own tale. "I'm going to check on Mama," she announced. *Then*, she thought, *I'll go and see Twist.*

Doctor Burton grunted a reply. When his attention was on a tray of cakes, Emma slipped from the table. She spotted Mister Jenkins three chairs down, surrounded by young ladies. Obviously delighted by their attention, the clerk was waving as if telling an exciting sea story. Shielding her face with her hat so he wouldn't see her, Emma hurried from the main cabin.

The outside air was refreshing, and she breathed deeply. The wind ruffled her hair and she dangled her hat over the railing. A sudden gust of wind almost sent it into the night. *If I let it go, would it fly upriver all the way to Papa?* Emma wondered. She missed her father so much.

The miners tell tales of gold nuggets the size of fists, he'd written in his last letter. *Prospectors are growing rich. Business men are finding new opportunities. I think of you every day, my precious wife and daughter. Together we will head to California, which holds the promise of fortune for all.*

A stateroom door opened behind her, and light spilled onto the veranda. Emma yanked back her hat, startled. She remembered her mother's sharp words: *young girls do not wander unescorted.* She sighed, feeling torn. Like Papa, she longed for adventure. Yet she didn't want Mama to fret.

Escaping from the light, she trotted down the walkway. The door to their stateroom was closed. She opened it slowly, peering inside. An oil lamp cast a golden glow. "Mama?"

"Emma?" her mother whispered from the bottom berth. Emma shut the door, set her hat on a hook, and tiptoed toward the bed. Mama pushed herself into a sitting position, and Emma plumped the pillow behind her.

"Are you all right, darling?" Mama asked as she ran her hand over her daughter's unruly curls. "You look as if you were tossed by a storm."

"I'm fine, Mama. I was in the pilothouse with Captain Digby and Mister LaBarge. Did you know we almost ran over a raft?"

"Almost ran over a raft?" Mama sank onto the pillows. "Do not tell me these stories, Emma. They make my heart sink. Oh, why did I consent to this journey?"

"But Mama, we *must* be with Papa. It's been ages and I miss him so." Emma kneeled on the floor. Her mother had always been strong and brave. The past month, though, she'd been sickly and anxious, and Emma was growing impatient.

"I know, dearest. I miss your father as much as you do, and I'm eager to reach him before..." Mama's voice trailed off.

Emma frowned. "Before what?"

"Before the creaking and shaking of this boat drive me batty," Mama said quickly. "But I must not bother you with my worries. You are just a child. Is Doctor Burton keeping you safe?"

"Yes, ma'am. As are Mister Jenkins and Captain Digby," Emma fibbed, not wanting to vex her mother further. "And I'm not a child," she added.

"Is that so?" Mama smiled and Emma was glad to see her happy again. Perhaps she was feeling better. But then her mother laid her arm over her eyes as if the light from the lantern hurt them. Abruptly, her head tipped sideways.

"Mama!" Emma jumped up. "Where's Kathleen?" she asked.

Just then, the door leading into the main cabin opened, and the servant girl stepped into the room carrying a tray.

"Kathleen, why did you leave my mother?" Emma demanded.

"I was fetchin' her supper, miss," Kathleen said.

"A waiter can bring her meals."

Kathleen bobbed her head.

"She is feeling faint, I think," Emma said.

"Yes, miss," the Irish girl said. "I'll see to her."

Emma glanced back at her mother. Mama gave Emma a weak smile and waved her away. "I'll be fine, sweetheart," she said. "Go."

"Yes, Mama," Emma said. When Kathleen bent to set down the tray, Emma opened her small trunk and found Twist's brush. She stuck it in her empty pocket. Before she left the room, she looked back at her mother one last time and saw that she was sleeping.

The veranda walkway was dark except for an occasional lantern hanging from a hook. Everyone was in the main cabin, dining. Afterward, there would be music and dancing. No one would miss her.

Emma glanced toward the bow and the stairway to the main deck. This was her chance.

Proper young ladies do not go below. She shook off the thought and headed down the walkway.

Emma knew from Captain Digby that the steamboat's boilers, cargo, and livestock were on the main deck. She knew it held the deckhands' living quarters, too. But Emma wasn't interested in any of that. All she wanted was to see Twist.

She would avoid the engineers at the boilers. She would steer past the firemen and the wood-burning furnaces. And wasn't she far too clever to get caught like nosy Harry Bixby?

Yes. Emma broke into a run, her boots thudding on the wooden walkway. She didn't stop until she'd reached the stairway. This time, she didn't hesitate on the top landing. Without looking back, she clattered down the steps into the dangers of the main deck.

CHAPTER FIVE

Emma froze at the bottom of the stairs. A deckhand stood on the bow, lighting the pine knots in a torch basket. They sizzled and spit, then began to flame. When he moved to the next one, she skittered behind a stack of cotton bales.

Heart thumping, she peered around. The burning torch baskets, which slanted over the water, cast a confusing web of shadows from the lines, rails, poles, and booms.

Emma shivered in the chill night air. She had no lantern, no candle, no shawl, and no notion where Twist might be. This had been a foolish idea, she now realized.

The deckhand swung around, heading toward her hiding place. She said a silent prayer for courage and darted from the bales to a cluster of barrels. When she crouched beside them, a voice hissed, "Be gone. No room 'ere."

Emma started. In the glow of the torchlights, she made out two figures: a man and woman huddled between the barrels. A worn-out blanket covered the woman's shoulders. Beneath the folds, a baby whimpered hungrily.

"Pardon me," Emma whispered. Crouching, she hurried toward the back of the boat, past more cargo piled high and neat. She paused to get her bearings. A lone lantern hung from a peg on a wooden pillar. In its circle of light, two deckhands were playing a dice game. Suddenly a quarrel arose, and one man leaped to his feet, a knife flashing in his hand. Emma gasped as he slashed at the other man's arm, ripping the sleeve. Then both men fled into the shadows.

She pressed against a crate, her pulse racing. Something sharp pecked the back of her neck. She spun around. The beady eye of a rooster glared at her from the slatted crate. Cocking his head, he ruffled his feathers angrily.

Emma crept away, following the path of the quarreling deckhands. A blast of heat hit the side of her face. In the light of the flames, she saw bare-chested firemen throwing logs into the boiler. Their skin gleamed with sweat.

One of the firemen paused to stare at her. His skin and eyes glowed red, making him look like a demon from one of Preacher Hobson's sermons. Emma gulped and hurried from the roar of the fire. Beyond the boilers, she heard other sounds: coughing, murmuring, a lullaby sung in a strange language.

As Emma's eyes adjusted to the dim light, she noticed that every nook and cranny was filled with people. They were stretched out on trunk tops, squeezed between boxes, hunkered behind hogsheads. Two little girls swaddled in rags slept in a coil of ropes. A woman wearing a shabby scarf sat on the top of a wooden crate. A toddler lay across her lap, chewing a crust of bread. A man walked by Emma, carrying a bucket. She pinched her nose at the stench.

Immigrants. Or, as Doctor Burton called them, *riffraff.* She'd seen them board the *Sally May* earlier, but she hadn't given them another thought.

A mounded blanket next to Emma's feet wiggled as if alive. Beside her, a woman propped against a trunk pleaded, "Miss, can you spare a sip of water?"

Emma backed away. Then she realized how priggish she was acting. Mama believed in alms for the poor and pity for the foreigners. Besides, this woman might know where to find Twist.

"I'm sorry, but I have none," Emma said to the

shawl-covered gray head. She was careful not to get too close, wary of lice and fleas. "Ma'am, do you know where the animals are stabled?"

The woman pointed a bony finger aft.

"Thank you." On Emma's left, a potbellied stove smoked. Twenty or more immigrants were huddled around it. They murmured to each other in languages that Emma didn't recognize. At the St. Louis School for Girls, she'd only studied French and Latin.

Emma hurried past, finding more cargo beyond the ring of stove light. A pinch of fear made her tremble. She hugged her arms against her chest, suddenly realizing that she was lost. She sidled behind a crate, not wanting to attract attention. At any moment the immigrants might rise up, steal her boots and apples, and toss her overboard.

Panic filled her. She'd never find Twist in this shadowy maze. She needed to get out. But which way was back to the stairs? Then Emma heard the loveliest sound in the world: the low of a cow. Hopeful once more, she made her way toward the sound. It was dark, but she could tell by the stomp of hooves and the smell of manure that she was close to the livestock. Reaching out, she felt the rough, slatted boards of a pen. A slimy nose tickled her fingers and a hog grunted. How was she going to find Twist in this sea of animals?

"Twist?" she called, hoping that her pony might hear her voice. "Twist?" she called again as she moved aft, using the boards to guide her.

A high-pitched whinny rang from somewhere in the midst of the animals. Tears sprang into Emma's eyes as she hurried toward the neigh. The backs and heads of the animals were silhouetted against the light of the lanterns. Emma spotted the wide horns of oxen and the giant ears of mules, but no horses. Where was her pony?

"Twist!" she called again. A fuzzy black muzzle poked over a top board. "Thank heaven, it's you!" Emma began to cry as she climbed blindly into the pen, not caring if she landed on a piglet or milk cow. She dropped down next to her pony, who whickered furiously. "I'm so glad I finally found you. Are you all right?"

Clasping her arms around Twist's neck, Emma hugged him tightly. Then she ran her hands from his withers to his flanks, making sure he wasn't hurt. He seemed to be fine. She looked around her. Twist was indeed in his own stall. But it was so tiny that the pony couldn't move front to back or side to side, much less turn around. And even if there had been room, the pony's head was tied to the front board with a rope in a tangled knot.

"Oh, Twist. You must long for your huge stall and grassy paddock at home," Emma said. "At least someone bedded this pen with straw," she added as she inched her way toward the front. "But where is your water bucket? Your grain? You must be thirsty and hungry."

Trying to find the bucket, she ducked under Twist's neck. The toe of her boot hit a lump that yelled, "Get off me, ye sot!"

Emma screamed as a figure rose from the straw and a scarecrow of a boy glared at her. She jerked herself upright. "Get off *you?*" she said. "What gall! This is my pony's private stall, not a gutter rat's bed." She gave him a hard kick.

"Ow!" The boy threw up his hands to shield himself. "Stop!"

Emma stopped, but she kept her foot aimed at him. In the dim light she could see that he wasn't much older than she. He wore a threadbare red-checked jacket. Its sleeves were too short, and the denims that barely reached below his knees were patched.

"What are you doing in here?" she demanded.

"What's it look like to ye?" he shot back.

Her mouth dropped open. She'd expected a meek reply. "It looks like you're stealing my pony's bed!"

"Stealing?" He snorted. "Yer wee horse invited me to share the stall."

"He did no such thing."

"He did." As if to show her the boy was telling the truth, Twist snuffled at the straw poking from his reddish brown hair.

"Well, he only likes you because you smell like a horse." Emma wrinkled her nose to prove her point.

At that, the boy scrambled to his bare feet, his fists clenched. Emma shrank behind the safety of Twist's head.

"Don't worry," he snapped. "I wouldn't hit a girl. Me mum taught me manners."

"Good," Emma said. "I'd hate to think my pony invited a *ruffian* to share his stall." She cocked her head as he brushed off his tattered trousers and jacket. "What are you doing back here with the animals?"

"No room anywhere else." He patted Twist with genuine fondness. "We were sleeping good 'til some lass started shouting, 'Twist! Twist!'" He imitated Emma's voice perfectly. "Her yelling could've waked me dead grandmum."

Emma bristled. This boy was not only smelly, but also very cheeky. "And did you pay passage for these sleeping quarters?" she asked.

Even in the near-dark, she could see the shift of his eyes.

"I knew it. You're a *stowaway*." Emma said the word half in disgust, half in awe at his daring. "I read about stowaways in *My Boys' and Girls' Magazine and Fireside Companion*. They sneak onto a boat and—"

"Hush now," he said, jerking his thumb toward the lantern light. "Or the engineers will hear ye and toss me off this ship. Look, I did ye a favor. Yer pony had no water. I found a bucket and dipped some from the river. He drank as if he was empty."

Emma softened. "Thank you, um…"

"Patrick. Me name is Patrick O'Brien."

"Pleased to meet you, Patrick. My name is Emma Wright and my pony's name is Licorice Twist. Because he's so black and sweet." Patrick gave her such a blank look that she knew he'd never heard of the candy, let alone tasted it.

Twist nuzzled her side. "Oh, I almost forgot, my precious, I brought you a treat." She pulled an apple from her pocket and fed it to the pony. As Twist crunched on the fruit, Emma glanced sideways at the boy. He was staring at the apple, licking his lips. "I have another one." She handed it to him, careful not to touch his dirty palm. He bit into it and chewed slowly, his eyes closed as if enjoying every morsel.

"I guess stowaways don't get food," she said.

He stopped chewing and squared his shoulders. "I won't be a stowaway for long. I aim to work off me passage." He pointed at the knot tied in Twist's rope. "I'm practicing me sailor knots."

"I know Captain Digby and Mister LaBarge, the pilot," Emma said, "Perhaps I can put in a good word."

"Thank ye, but I need to join the crew without the captain knowing I snuck on board. I don't want them throwing me and me sis—" Abruptly he stopped talking and took another bite of apple.

"Your sister?" Emma said in surprise. "She's a stowaway, too?"

"No," he said, climbing up the boards that formed the pen wall. "I'll be off now."

"Wait!"

He stopped but didn't look back at her.

"Perhaps we can come to an agreement," Emma called. "I need someone to look after Twist. It pains me to learn he had no water." She pulled the brush from her pocket. "And he's used to having a clean stall and being groomed every day. Surely you'd rather sleep here than with the pigs?"

The boy looked at her, the lantern light full on his face. Emma realized he might be a stowaway, but he had fair features and an agreeable, honest look about him. "Perhaps we could make a deal?"

He frowned. "Like what? Ye don't tell the captain or the mate I'm a stowaway, and I don't tell him a cabin passenger is below where her don't belong?"

"Um, no. You'll get to share Twist's stall in return for caring for him."

"I ain't no stable boy," he said, sulking.

"I could bring you food."

Patrick arched one brow, as if interested. Finally, he nodded. "Deal, then." He dropped back into the stall, holding out his hand to shake. Emma shrank from the gesture—no servant or hired worker had ever dared offer his hand to her.

"Deal," she said quickly. "Now, as for Twist's care and feeding..." She launched into a list of long-winded instructions.

"And in return for me service, I fancy porkpie topped off with a mash," Patrick demanded when she finished, as if *he* was the master and not the worker.

"You'll get whatever I can hide in my pinafore pocket," Emma said, "whenever I can sneak below. The third clerk thinks he has to keep an eye on me."

Patrick nodded as if he understood what she was going through. "'Tis best to do it at night, then."

"I'd best head off before Doctor Burton sends out a

search party," Emma said. "He thinks he has to keep an eye on me, too."

"Too many eyes on you, I'd say," Patrick said with a grin. Emma had to agree.

She said good-bye to Twist and climbed from the pen, careful not to let her skirts rise up over her knee when she swung her legs over the highest slat.

"Miss Emma, want me to walk with ye to the cabin stairs?" Patrick asked politely.

Emma paused. He *was* being gentlemanly. And an escort through the riffraff might be safest.

"I would like that. Do you know the way?"

"Aye." He clambered up the boards again like a squirrel, jumping down on the other side before Emma's boot toe touched the floor.

"Come," he said, gesturing for her to follow.

Emma kept close to him as he wound his way toward the bow. She tried to remember the route so she wouldn't get lost on her next visit. If she expected Patrick to keep his word, she needed to keep hers.

He stopped behind the barrels and pointed to the torch-lighted bow. Emma smiled a thank-you. She was about to step from her hiding place when the pounding of feet on wood made her freeze.

Coming down the stairs were half a dozen waiters

carrying pans piled high with food. Behind the waiters, she saw Mister Jenkins carrying a ledger.

Emma bit back a scream. If the mud clerk caught her on the main deck she was done for. He'd tell Doctor Burton who would tell Captain Digby, and just like Harry Bixby, she would be cast ashore at the next stop!

CHAPTER SIX

Grub pile! Grub pile!" the waiters chanted as they headed straight toward Emma.

Deckhands seemed to appear from nowhere. They carried tin cups, spoons, and wooden slabs. In the middle strode the first mate. He swung his gnarled stick, knocking all others from his path so he would reach the food first.

Patrick grabbed Emma's wrist and pulled her back the way they had come. The hungry deckhands swarmed past, threatening to trample them.

Dropping on all fours, Emma and Patrick scrambled beneath a canvas sheet stretched like a curtain between two pillars. Boots and bare feet narrowly missed tromping on Emma as she pulled her legs under the canvas.

When she dared to look up, she saw tiers of narrow bunks. The crew's sleeping quarters, she guessed. The area was now empty, but it would soon be filled again when the deckhands brought back their grub.

"This way," Patrick whispered. Like mice, they scurried under another canvas and alongside a stack of crates. Patrick stopped, peered around the last crate, and pointed ahead. Emma could see one of the torchlights on the bow. While the waiters and Mister Jenkins were busy giving out the food, she could make it safely up the stairs.

"Thank you," Emma told Patrick. She took one last look around before hopping to her feet and sprinting toward the bow. She rounded the corner and flew up the stairs and out of the cabin. She didn't slow to catch her breath until she reached the veranda.

Music came from the main cabin. The two girls from the ladies' parlor were strolling down the walkway toward her. Each was accompanied by an older woman. If they saw Emma, they would wonder about her lack of a chaperone. And if the news reached Doctor Burton or her mother, she'd be forever forbidden to go off on her own.

Emma bolted in the opposite direction, found the door to her stateroom, and threw it open. In the faint light from the kerosene lamp, she could see Kathleen sitting on a stool next to Mama's berth, her head slumped over. Emma closed the door, and the maid's chin quickly snapped up. "I only nodded off for a wee moment, miss," she said, jumping to her feet.

"Is my mother feeling better, Kathleen?"

"Yes, miss." Kathleen hurried over and poured some water into the washbowl. "Let me help ye wash up." She handed Emma a bar of soap. "I laid out yer nightgown."

"Thank you." As Emma scrubbed, she glanced at Mama, who was sleeping peacefully. Then she thought about the day, and her heart began thumping excitedly.

Papa had been right: this river journey was full of adventure! Her friends at St. Louis School for Girls would be glittery-eyed with envy. Their tea parties and parlor games were dull in comparison. Best of all, she'd found that her beloved Twist was doing well, and she'd even met a stowaway named Patrick.

As Emma dried her face, she couldn't help but smile. She'd fooled Doctor Burton and Mister Jenkins. Neither had a whit of an idea that she'd gone to the forbidden main deck. Tomorrow she'd have to risk being caught again. Patrick would need food and Twist would need hugs. But for now, she—and her secrets— were safe.

* * *

Emma paced the carpet of the ladies' parlor. For two very long days, she'd been trapped in the company of those two annoying girls Josephine and Julia, as well as their mothers Mrs. Hanover and Mrs. Ringwald. There had been no chance of going below to the hurricane deck or up to the pilothouse. Doctor Burton surely had no idea she'd snuck to the main deck the other day, but he seemed to be punishing her anyway.

Emma was worried about Patrick and Twist. At supper, she'd stuffed the pockets of her pinafore with bread, sausage, cheese, apples, and nuts in hopes that tonight she could get away. She'd wrapped the sausage in her napkin, but already the grease had soaked into her dress.

"Emma, it's your turn," Julia said from the other side of the checkerboard.

"Yes, please sit, dear," Mrs. Ringwald said. "You're wearing out the carpet."

"And your stomping back and forth is quite unbecoming to a young lady," Mrs. Hanover added.

Without a word, Emma slouched into her chair and pushed her red checker two squares.

"King me!" Julia declared. Emma plunked the only

black checker of Julia's that she had captured on top. Then she crossed her arms and frowned, wishing she was anyplace else.

"You look like a deckhand, Emma," Julia said. "Grunting and scowling like that."

Mrs. Hanover gave her daughter a sharp look. "And how would you know about the deckhands?"

"We can see them over the railing," Julia said quickly.

Josephine giggled. "Sometimes they smile up at us."

"Josephine!" Mrs. Ringwald placed the back of her hand on her forehead in alarm. "Do you want to find a suitable husband one day?"

"Yes, Mama."

"Then act like a proper lady."

Emma didn't listen to any more of this boring conversation. She had important things to think about. Tomorrow the *Sally May* was scheduled to stop at Jefferson City. What if Patrick was getting off? What if he hadn't been caring for Twist all this time?

Emma chewed her lip, growing frantic with worry. Suddenly she sprang from the chair, announcing, "Excuse me. I need to check on my mother."

"But I was about to win," Julia protested.

"You're excused, my dear," Mrs. Ringwald said to

Emma. "However, you must go directly to your state-room. Doctor Burton's orders. Do you understand? Young ladies do *not* run wild." She gave her own daughter a stern look.

"Yes, ma'am," Emma said politely before hurrying away.

"I'm glad *she's* gone," she heard Josephine say. "So snooty. And did you notice she smelled like sausage?"

Instead of going to the stateroom, Emma made a beeline to the main deck. She found her way past the immigrants, deckhands, and roustabouts who seemed to occupy every nook. No wonder Patrick was bunking with the livestock.

This time she didn't get lost. When she reached Twist's stall, the pony poked his nose over the top board and wiggled his upper lip. "Hello, my precious!" Emma greeted him. "Did you miss me?"

"I surely did." A face popped up next to Twist's. "Nearly starved, I am. All these days I been feeding and brushing yer horse like he belongs to the Queen of England, and ye don't show up with one bite fer me."

"I couldn't," Emma said. "Doctor Burton had two ladies watching me like hawks eyeing a rabbit."

"Rabbit?" A grubby hand, palm up, slid over the top slat. "Give it here. I like it fried, roasted, stewed—"

"Mind your manners, please." Emma climbed up the side of the pen. When she swung her leg over, her petticoat caught on the top. Unsnagging the lacy hem, she climbed down next to Twist.

Hungry lips smacked beside her. "Do I smell sausage?"

Emma whirled. Up close, Patrick's face seemed even dirtier than before, and he reeked of the hogs penned nearby. "Don't you ever wash?" she snapped.

"Why yes, m'lady. Me servant filled a hot tub last night and scrubbed me down." His gaze dove to her pocket. "Hurry before I keel over from hunger."

Emma pulled out some of the food. He snatched the sausage, barely unwrapping it before shoving the whole thing in his mouth. "Weren't you taught to chew slowly?" she asked.

He laughed, the sound muffled by the mouthful of sausage, then swallowed. "In me family? I would have starved."

"Where *is* your family?" Emma asked, feeding Twist an apple.

He shrugged. "Me mum is dead. And me da…" He shrugged. Crouching in the corner by Twist's bucket, he wolfed down the cheese and bread she had brought.

"My father's in Kansas City," Emma said. "We're

meeting him and traveling upriver to St. Joseph. From there we're going to California to find gold." Patrick's eyes lit up at the word *gold*, but he kept eating. Emma found Twist's brush on the ground by the bucket. "Do you have brothers and *sisters*?" she asked, remembering his earlier slip.

"A whole flock of 'em."

Emma couldn't imagine a large family. She was an only child with a bedroom all to herself and two parents to spoil her.

"Aidan, Kevin, Nial, and Ronan are the oldest," Patrick recited. "Me and me sister are the youngest. Me brothers are still in Ireland with families and woes of their own. When Mum died, they already had too many mouths to feed. So..." His voice trailed away.

"So then you set out for America? Just you and your sister?"

"Just me," he said quickly.

"How brave." Emma ran her hand along Twist's neck, fascinated by Patrick's story. "So where is your sister now?"

Patrick didn't answer. "Me gut's still rumbling. What else do ye have stashed in those pockets?"

Emma pulled out another apple. "I was going to give this to Twist. But since you're so hun—"

He snatched it from her. "I'll leave him the core."

"My, but you're generous," Emma said. "Though I must say, Twist's coat does look silky, and he has a bit of water and hay. I suppose you have earned your keep."

Patrick nodded. "I guard that bucket with me life so them Germans don't steal it to wash their babies."

"Thank you. I promise that next time I visit, I'll bring more for you to eat."

He polished off the apple, fed Twist the core, and began to lick the sausage grease from his fingers.

Emma busied herself brushing Twist's mane. She'd never really talked to a boy before, especially one so dirty and ill-mannered.

"So what's it like up on the cabin deck?" Patrick asked. "Do ye get sausage and bread every day?"

"Every day." She didn't list the other endless meal choices.

"Where do ye sleep?"

"My mother and I share a stateroom. During the day, we spend most of our time in the main cabin. The gentlemen play cards and smoke. In the parlor, the ladies read and gossip. At night there's music and dancing."

Patrick stopped licking his fingers and stared at her. Emma decided not to tell him about Kathleen and the other maids who emptied the chamber pots and washbasins. Or about the waiters who served the guests all day and played music all night for their pleasure. Instead she told him a funny story.

"One of the passengers, Missus Thornrose, carries her poodle everywhere. This morning, when the *Sally May* backed from the woodyard, the poodle leaped from her arms. It must have seen a rabbit on shore because it jumped over the veranda railing and fell into the river. By the hullabaloo, you would have thought Missus Thornrose had fallen in."

"So that's the ruckus I heard," Patrick said.

"The poodle would have been lost except the first mate jumped into the water and saved it. Wasn't that brave? The deckhands threw him a rope and hauled him and pup aboard. Of course, Missus Thornrose rewarded him with a gold coin."

Patrick frowned. "Ye want to hear me own story?" he asked, his shoulders hunched in the red jacket. "Early this same morning, I was helping at that same landing. 'Woodpile! Woodpile!' the mate hollers before the sun's barely up. They need strong arms to carry the wood on board, and the captain offered me two bits to help. Four logs at a time, I carried. Two on each shoulder."

Emma gave him an admiring look although she'd seen many of the roustabouts carrying six.

"The gangplank's narrow and slippery, and the man in front of me fell into the river. Dropped like a stone and disappeared without a cry. Do ye think the brave first mate dove in after him?"

"Why, of course," Emma said.

Patrick shook his head. "'Ah, leave him, he's just a bloody Irishman.' That's what the first mate said."

Emma stopped brushing. "What happened?"

"The Irishman couldn't swim. What do you think happened?"

"You mean he drowned?"

Patrick shrugged, which seemed to be his response for just about everything he didn't care to answer. "Do *you* know how to swim?" Emma asked him.

He cut his eyes from her.

"I'll teach you then," Emma said. "When we get to Jefferson City. That's our next stop."

He rose to his feet. "You'll not be teaching me nothing," he said gruffly. "By then, I'll be working full-time with the roustabouts." He pointed to Twist's rope. "I've been practicing me knots, and one day I'll be a deckhand. Then I'll save enough money to travel to the gold mines, too."

"But you're just a boy."

Patrick scowled. "A *boy* don't earn his own way,

miss." Picking up the bucket, he plunked it at Emma's feet. Water spilled over her boots. "Tend yer own pony from now on," he said. Then he grabbed the top board and vaulted from Twist's pen.

CHAPTER SEVEN

"Patrick!" Emma called. She heard the thump of his bare feet on the floor and saw the flash of a red sleeve. Then he disappeared among the animals.

Twist nudged her side. She turned around and scratched the white star on the pony's nose. "What a wretch," she muttered. "He breaks our deal, speaks to me curtly, and soaks my boots. Then he runs off like he has hot cinders in his pants. Just because I called him a *boy*."

But he was a boy, wasn't he? He couldn't be more than eleven or twelve. Alexander Renshaw, who lived on their street in St. Louis, was about that age. His mama accompanied him everywhere, and he still wore his hair in long curls.

Emma began grooming Twist again. "No matter. He's only a gutter rat. That's what Cousin Minna would call

him. Besides, I can take care of you myself." She leaned
back to admire Twist's shiny coat, then looked down at
the empty bucket. Patrick had dipped water from the
river. How difficult could that be?

She was picking up the bucket when Twist raised his
tail. Steamy manure plopped to the straw. Emma
pinched her nose shut. At home in St. Louis, her job was
riding and petting Twist. It was Mister Tommy's job to
keep the stable spotless. Emma had never seen him clean
a stall, but she knew he used a pitchfork, which she certainly didn't have.

"Oh, I wish Mister Tommy were here," Emma grumbled. The door to the pen was at Twist's tail end. Still
holding her nose, Emma squeezed her way around the
pony's flank. A cord was tied around the post and door
frame, holding it secure. The cord was knotted on the
outside, so Emma couldn't open the door from where
she stood.

Draping the bucket handle over her arm, she climbed
from the stall. When she jumped down on the other
side, she stumbled into the bony side of a cow. The animal swatted her with its ropy tail.

Several oxen were tied near the door to Twist's pen.
Emma edged past them and then wound her way
between the other pens to the outside edge of the deck.

The air was chilly away from the warmth of the animals. Shivering, she stared over the edge, which had no railing. A foot below her, the river flowed inky and cold. She was wondering how to fill the bucket when a skeletal hand rose from the water.

With a scream, she jumped back, her heart thudding. Was it the drowned Irishman Patrick had told her about? Could he still be alive? She forced herself to peer closer, then saw that the bent fingers were only twigs on a branch. *Silly goose,* she told herself.

Setting down the bucket, Emma stretched out flat, belly down, on the deck. Grasping the rope handle, she carefully dipped the bucket into the river. The pull of the water almost dragged her overboard, but she managed to hang on. Even though the bucket was only half full, she could barely lift it.

This is folly, Emma thought. The river that would lead her to Papa might also take her away from him forever. She could swim, but Patrick was the only person who knew she was on the main deck. If she fell in, she'd be as lost as the Irishman.

But Twist needed water, and she couldn't count on Patrick, Doctor Burton, Captain Digby, Mister Jenkins, or the first mate to care for her pony.

Emma gritted her teeth and hauled the bucket onto

the deck, spilling water everywhere. She scrambled to her feet. The front of her pinafore was wet and streaked with dirt. As she carried the water back to the pen, her boots squished and the bucket banged against her side.

When she reached Twist's pen, she stopped dead. One of the oxen had lain down in front of the stall, its mountainous back pressed tightly against the door. Emma's shoulders sagged. She would never be able to budge such a beast. And she wasn't strong enough to climb into the pen carrying the bucket. "Pox on you, Patrick O'Brien," she muttered. It was completely his fault.

She swiped tears of frustration from her eyes, determined not to give up. "Good day, Mister Ox," she said cheerfully. "May I use you as stairs?"

Without waiting for the beast's reply, Emma stepped onto the ox's hind end. Quickly, she scrambled high onto its slippery back. Then, with a grunt, she heaved the bucket over the door.

Suddenly, the huge animal rose to its feet, hoisting Emma into the air. The bucket dropped to the stall floor as she tumbled into the pen. She landed hard against the side wall, her legs under Twist's belly. Dazed, she lay there for a second.

Twist peered curiously at her. "I'm all right," Emma

told him as she tested out her arms. They would be sore but no bones were broken. Her gaze went to the bucket and she sighed with relief. Not all the water had been lost.

With her back propped against the wall, she pushed to her feet. Then she inched around to Twist's tail, stepping in the manure. Grimacing, she dragged the bucket to the pony's head.

Emma blew out a weary breath. It was late, and she was bruised and battered. Even worse, tomorrow she would have to do this all over again.

The thought made her fume. Then she came up with an idea. Perhaps she could wheedle a coin out of Doctor Burton. Then she could pay one of the other immigrants to watch over Twist. Surely they would be grateful for the job. But could she trust another stranger to care for her pony?

No. She'd have to come up with a different plan. Maybe Kathleen could be persuaded. Emma could watch over Mama while the maid cared for Twist.

As Twist drank, Emma patted him good-bye. "I'll think of something," she told him.

Moments later, she was trotting along the veranda toward her stateroom. There were no sounds coming from the main cabin, and most of the lanterns had been snuffed. Emma knew it was past her proper bedtime. She prayed that Mama would be asleep and Doctor Burton was still away gambling.

When she reached the stateroom, she eased open the door and listened. She heard soft breathing. Hurrah, her mother *was* asleep. All she needed to do was sneak inside, change into her nightgown, and toss her ruined clothes overboard.

But as she stepped into the stateroom, her wet boot hit a bulky mound stretched across the doorway. Pitching over it, Emma landed hard on the floor.

"Sorry, miss!" Kathleen rose from where she'd been lying. A blanket covered her shoulders like a shawl, and she blinked sleepily at Emma.

Emma put a finger to her lips, her gaze flying to the lower berth. "Shhh. I don't want to wake Mama."

"Ah, yer mum won't wake. She took a dose of sarsaparilla." Kathleen clutched the blanket tighter. "What're ye doing coming in so late?" she whispered. "Are ye all right?"

Emma frowned. She wasn't about to explain her whereabouts to a servant. "I'm fine." But she wasn't. Her palms stung where she'd caught herself and her limbs now had bumps on top of the bruises. "What are *you* doing lying in front of the door?" she asked.

Kathleen looked flustered. "That's where I sleep every night. I did not mean to trip ye."

"No matter." Emma stood up, shivering, cold in her damp clothes. "Bring me some wash water, please."

"Yes, miss." Kathleen dropped the blanket. She was still wearing her uniform. Plucking her cap from a peg, she placed it on her tousled hair, which had escaped from its bun.

"There's still some warm water," Kathleen said, pouring half a pitcher into the bowl. "We'll get ye washed in no time. As for yer dress and pinafore..." Her voice trailed off as she cast a sidelong glance at Emma.

"Could you fetch me a cup of hot cocoa, too? Get two cups, one for you," Emma said, wanting Kathleen to go away. The maid's gaze was much too curious.

"Yes, miss." Kathleen hurried from the stateroom, being careful to close the door quietly behind her.

Emma stripped to her chemise and scrubbed her filthy hands, neck, and face. She tossed the gray, soapy water into the chamber pot and poured fresh water into the bowl to rinse.

Mama moaned in her sleep, making Emma jump. What if her mother woke up? What story could she invent to explain her wet clothes and lateness?

I fell overboard and a deckhand saved me.

It had worked for Missus Thornrose's poodle.

By the time Kathleen came back carrying two steaming mugs, Emma was dressed in her nightgown. "My pinafore, stockings, and dress need to be washed," she told the maid. "And my boots cleaned and polished."

"Yes, miss." Kathleen handed her the hot chocolate.

Emma sat gingerly on the end of the berth. Her mother didn't stir. As Emma blew on the steaming cocoa, she studied the Irish girl, who leaned wearily against the wall and sipped from her own cup. Kathleen's cap was askew and auburn curls framed her face. Had Doctor Burton enlisted the young maid's help? Maybe the doctor had given her a coin to tattle on Emma.

"Is yer chocolate all right, miss?" Kathleen asked, alarm sharpening her face when she caught Emma staring at her. "I can fetch ye another."

Yer chocolate? Fetch ye another? Emma suddenly realized that Kathleen had the same color hair and way of speaking as Patrick. Their eyes were similar, too.

"No, this is delicious. And yours?" Emma asked.

"Oh, 'tis a treat." The maid sighed with delight.

"You've never had hot chocolate before?"

Kathleen shrugged, as if embarrassed.

Emma's eyes widened at the familiar gesture. This girl had to be Patrick's sister!

CHAPTER EIGHT

Kathleen, do you have a brother named Patrick?" The maid startled as if surprised by Emma's question. "I—"

Just then Emma's mother turned over and the quilt slipped to the side. Setting the mug on the edge of the washstand, Kathleen rushed to cover her up again.

"You do, don't you?" Emma said. "And he's a stowaway on the *Sally May*."

Kathleen's hands shook on the quilt. "Please don't tell anyone about me brother," she whispered, unable to meet Emma's gaze. "He's a good lad and clever. I hired on to work, but the clerk said Patrick was too young. If anyone discovers he's a stowaway, he'll be put ashore."

"Don't worry. I won't tell."

"Thank ye." Kathleen bustled over to the pile of dirty clothes. "I'll get these washed tonight, miss, and set them by the stove in the parlor. Then they'll have a chance to dry."

When Kathleen left, Emma finished her hot chocolate. A Cousin Minna–type idea was flitting through her mind. Tomorrow she'd find Patrick and tell him she knew his secret—that his sister was her mother's maid.

Then she would inform him that if he didn't keep taking care of Twist, she'd tell Captain Digby he was a stowaway. That should change Patrick's rude behavior.

The plan pleased Emma. She finished her cocoa, then pulled herself into the upper berth. Tiredness swept over her. As she slid her aching limbs under the quilt, she smiled at her clever plan to make sure Twist would be cared for. Cousin Minna would be proud of the sneaky way Emma had solved the problem.

But as Emma rolled onto her side, guilt pricked her. She wasn't bossy and snooty like Cousin Minna. And she'd promised Kathleen she wouldn't tell her secret. But Twist needed hay and water. Perhaps tomorrow, a better plan would come to her. Tonight, however, all she could think of was sleep.

* * *

"Careful, Mama." Emma held her mother's elbow as they slowly climbed the steps to the hurricane deck.

"Yes, Missus Wright, please watch yer step," Kathleen said behind them.

"Almost there," Mister Jenkins said from above.

It was late morning and the sun shone brightly. Emma had finally convinced her mother that fresh air, not medicine, would clear her head. Doctor Burton had not been in favor of the plan. Or maybe he'd been too deep in his cards to care, Emma wasn't sure which. But at breakfast, Captain Digby had agreed that the marvelous breezes on the hurricane deck were just what Mama needed and had sent Mister Jenkins to assist them.

When they finally reached the hurricane deck, Emma said, "Isn't the river breathtaking?"

Beside her, Mama nodded, but her face was greenish. "Yes, Emma," she said as she opened a parasol. "You and Captain Digby were correct. The sun and air are delightful."

With Kathleen on one side and Emma on the other, Mama let them steer her to the railing, which she gripped tightly. Mister Jenkins bid them good day. "We will be landing at Jefferson City soon, so I must get back to work. There is cargo to be sorted."

"Thank you, Mister Jenkins," Mama said, sweat shimmering on her cheeks. She was overdressed in her best velvet cloak. White gloves and plumed hat finished her outfit. Emma wore her Sunday best, too—her everyday dress was still damp—and her straw hat to keep off the sun.

Doctor Burton was escorting Mama and Emma to shore for their stop at Jefferson City. Mama wanted to telegraph Papa, who was still days ahead of them. Emma was torn. Part of her needed a break from river travel. Another part wanted to check on Twist again while the steamboat was docked.

Emma left Mama in Kathleen's care and hurried after the mud clerk. "Mister Jenkins, could I speak to you a minute? Julia was saying what a good storyteller you are."

Mister Jenkins paused at the compliment. "How nice of Miss Julia to say such a thing," he said, beaming.

"She *raved*. I'd love to hear the tale of Harry Bixby when you get the chance."

"Harry Bixby?" Mister Jenkins frowned. "I don't believe I know that one."

"About the boy who disobeyed the ship rules and ventured below?" Emma prompted.

"No, sorry. But at dinner tonight and I'll tell you and Miss Julia about—"

But Emma had already turned to rush back to Mama. So much for Captain Digby and Mister LaBarge telling her the truth. There was no Harry Bixby, so nosy children weren't put off the *Sally May*. She would go into Jefferson City with Mama today. Tonight she'd sneak to the main deck.

And what about her plan? Did she have the heart to tell on Patrick? Perhaps if she only *pretended* she was going to tell the captain…

When Emma reached them, her mother was holding tight to the railing, her face still green. "Kathleen, did you bring Mama's handkerchief?" Emma asked.

The young maid was staring over the water, eyes wide with wonder. "Yes, miss. 'Tis here. In my pocket." Barely taking her gaze off the river, she handed the handkerchief to Emma's mother.

"You've not seen the river before?" Emma asked.

Kathleen shook her head. "Not since we boarded. The Mississippi is so grand."

"We're on the Missouri River now. Captain Digby said at breakfast that we'll reach Jefferson City soon if the water stays calm."

"Look, miss!" Kathleen pointed excitedly toward the shore. "I believe it's an Indian."

Emma looked where Kathleen was pointing. A lone man stood on a bluff. He had long black hair in braids and a robe wrapped around his shoulders. "Mama, Kathleen is right," Emma said. "But where are his feathers, bow and arrows, and war pony?" She'd read frightening stories of Indians in *My Boys' and Girls' Magazine and Fireside Companion*. "Perhaps he's signaling to a war party waiting up ahead to ambush us."

"Ambush us?" Mama frowned. She pressed the handkerchief to her lips. "I do wish your father would stop telling you such horrid stories."

The steamboat slowly chugged around a bend. Emma craned her neck, keeping her eye on the Indian, waiting for an attack. But none came. Instead, several ladies pounced upon Mama with greetings and expressions of concern: "Lovely day, isn't it, Missus Wright?" "How are you feeling, Missus Wright?" Emma quickly grew bored with their chatter. Excusing herself, she made her way to the pilothouse.

"Good day, Mister LaBarge," she greeted the pilot from the doorway. "Are we nearing Jefferson City?"

"Aye, we are, Miss Wright," he replied. "Are you ready to help me land this whale of a boat?"

"Yes, sir." She leaped up the last step and took hold of the wheel. Ahead of them, she could see Captain Digby on the Texas deck roof. He had a megaphone in one hand, preparing to shout directions for landing.

"Mister LaBarge, did you see the Indian on the hill?" Emma asked.

"Aye."

"Was he not preparing to attack us?"

He shook his head. "The Indians in this area won't attack. Too many of them have been wiped out by cholera and smallpox. Others starve on reservations because settlers have taken their land. The rest trade trinkets or beg food to survive."

Emma stared at him. Was this true? Then she cocked her head. "Are you telling me another tale?" she asked. "Like the one about Harry Bixby?"

The pilot chuckled. "So you caught on to us, then? But no, Miss Emma, the plight of the Indians along the river is no tale."

"Stop the boat!" Captain Digby suddenly hollered to Mister LaBarge, startling Emma.

Immediately the pilot rang two bells, one for each paddlewheel, then yelled back, "All stopped!"

"May I stand fore with Captain Digby?" Emma asked the pilot. He nodded, his attention on the landing.

Emma trotted across the roof to join the captain. Farms, shacks, and fences dotted the riverbank to the left, signaling that they were getting close to the town. Indeed, she could just make out Jefferson City, a cluster of buildings and houses separated by narrow streets. Townspeople crowded the landing like ants, waiting to board or to pick up mail and supplies. As the steamboat drew closer, they cheered.

"Back slow, larboard!" Captain Digby shouted.

Mister LaBarge rang the larboard stopping bell. "All stopped," the pilot called.

Slowly, the stern of the *Sally May* turned toward shore. Emma peered over the edge of the roof. Below, the deckhands waited, lines in their hands.

Emma watched as the *Sally May* edged closer to the landing. She aided Captain Digby by keeping watch, and finally, after many commands and much bell ringing, the *Sally May* was tied fast.

After thanking Captain Digby, Emma ran back to Mama. Kathleen was guiding her down the steps to the cabin deck.

"Wasn't that thrilling?" Emma exclaimed. "Mister LaBarge is a lightning pilot," she repeated Captain Digby's boast. "And I helped land the steamboat."

"That's nice, Emma," Mama said. "Now let's find Doctor Burton. I must go ashore and telegraph your father."

"I know where to find the doctor," Emma said. "I'll fetch him and we'll meet in the cabin circle, by the stairs leading to the main deck." She sidestepped around Mama, whose bell-shaped skirts nearly blocked the walkway.

Emma found the doctor in the gentlemen's area huddled over a hand of cards. "Why, you've a pair of aces," she said, peering over his shoulder. "I would place a large bet if I were you."

Sputtering with annoyance, he threw his cards face down. Around the table, the other players chuckled. "Good heavens, child," the doctor said, his cigar bobbling between his lips. "Can't you keep silent? You have just cost me a gold mine."

"Come." She tugged on his elbow. "You promised to escort Mama and me into town."

"Town?" Doctor Burton checked his pocket watch. "We're at Jefferson City already?"

"Yes, and Mama is eager to be on dry land."

"As am I." Doctor Burton pushed away from the table and rose. "Gentlemen, excuse me, but you have swindled me out of my last dollar for today."

He followed Emma to the cabin circle where Mama waited with Kathleen. Doctor Burton offered his elbow to Mrs. Wright, and they all went down the stairs. The main deck was teeming with passengers. Emma glanced around, wondering if Patrick might be unloading cargo with the roustabouts. Then she scolded herself. Why did that annoying boy keep popping into her thoughts?

She turned her mind to Twist instead. Here she was, getting a break from river travel, while he was still trapped in a tiny stall. If only she could let him out for fresh air and a bite of grass.

Doctor Burton paused at the bottom of the stairs. A crush of ragged immigrants surged toward the gangplank. "Missus Wright, I cannot jeopardize your safety in this unwashed mob. Let's wait a moment until the riffraff is past." He led them to an empty spot next to a stack of cotton bales. Emma stood in front of the doctor, eager to see everything. The smoke from his cigar swirled around her straw hat. She coughed loudly and not very politely.

Kathleen stood next to her, looking in all directions, as if just as curious. *Or,* Emma wondered, *is she searching for Patrick, too?*

"Kathleen, are you and your brother planning to leave the *Sally May* here at Jefferson?" Emma whispered, feeling a pinch of worry. If neither of them were on board, who would care for Twist and Mama?

"No, miss," Kathleen whispered back. "I'm quitting me job with the steamboat, all right, but I'm staying on until St. Joe. From there we'll head west to California like ye and yer family."

Emma was surprised. "Really? What will you do out west?"

"I will open a laundry. Miners need clean clothes. I'm thrifty, like me mum." Kathleen said proudly. "When I make enough money washing clothes, I'll open a boarding house."

"You can do that?" Emma had never heard of a young woman doing such a thing. Even one with a clever brother.

Kathleen nodded. "I certainly can, miss."

"Oh." Emma blinked. Now Kathleen sounded as prideful as Patrick. For a moment, she was envious. But she quickly shook away the feeling. How could she be jealous of a maid and a stowaway? Besides, she would soon be on her own adventure with Papa.

"The way is clear, ladies," Doctor Burton said, puffing his cigar. "Walk carefully across the gangplank." He guided Mama across the deck.

Emma started after them. Suddenly fingers clawed at her shoulder, pulling her back. "Miss Emma!" Kathleen cried out. "Yer hat's on fire!"

CHAPTER NINE

Emma froze. Sizzling sounds came from atop her head. Heat frizzled her hair. Kathleen grabbed the straw hat and threw it on the deck. It fell against a cotton bale. Flames licked at the cotton and ignited it.

Stunned, Emma stared at her burning hat.

"Get back, miss!" Kathleen pushed her aside and began stomping the hat. A spark jumped, catching the hem of her uniform, where it blazed up and flared like golden wings.

Emma gasped. "Fire!" she shouted, finally finding her voice.

Someone shoved past her and tossed a bucketful of water onto Kathleen's skirt. It was Patrick. "Get another one," he ordered Emma. He handed her the bucket, then knocked his sister to the damp deck and rolled her around. A roustabout grabbed the bucket from Emma's arms and ran for more water. Other workers rushed up to douse the smoldering cotton bale.

Emma helped Kathleen to her feet. "Are you all right?"

The maid was dazed and her hem charred, but she nodded. "Yes, miss. Thank ye for calling for help."

"Thank *you*, Kathleen, for swatting off my hat. I need to thank your brother as well." She nodded at Patrick, who was tossing another bucket of water on the cotton bales.

Just then the first mate bustled into the fray. "What numskull tried to burn up the boat?" he asked. He snatched up what was left of Emma's hat and waved it in her face, scowling. She shrank from the smoking brim and his furious glare. "Was it *you*, miss?"

Patrick stepped in front of Emma. "It were an ash," he said. "Probably from a man's cigar. It fell onto her hat. She is not to blame."

"It did happen that way, sir," Emma added meekly, thinking of Doctor Burton. Then she mustered some Cousin Minna courage and glanced at the first mate. "I would be a *numskull* to set my own hat on fire, wouldn't I?"

The man's frown deepened. Around them, deckhands and roustabouts had gathered, as if watching a play in the theater. Emma swallowed hard, waiting for him to order her off the boat. Or worse, flog Patrick for speaking up. But with a shrug, the mate threw the hat overboard.

"These boats are floating woodpiles," he said. "Everyone must be careful at all times." He jerked his thumb toward the roustabouts. "Now pop yer eyes back in yer turtleheads and get these bales unloaded," he told them, aiming his words toward Patrick as well. "This ain't a holiday."

Emma blew out a relieved breath. "Come, Kathleen, we must find Mama and Doctor Burton." Tilting her chin, she marched across the deck to the gangplank. All who had been watching must have thought her a puffed-up goose who needed rescuing by a maid and a boy.

Servants must obey us, Cousin Minna often said. Even if it meant risking their lives to save a silly girl from fire? Emma frowned. As she crossed the gangplank, she realized she hadn't thanked Patrick. But when she jumped onto the wharf and turned around, he had disappeared.

The landing was packed with people searching for family, workers unloading cargo, and townspeople pulling carts. Emma peered through the crowd, hunting for Mama's velvet cloak and Doctor Burton's top hat.

"Miss Emma!" the doctor's voice thundered over the

noise. "Come, child. You are giving your mother fits. She feared you were lost."

"Not lost, just on fire," Emma muttered to no one as she and Kathleen hurried toward the doctor. Mama stood next to him on the stoop of a building, a piece of paper in her hand. Was it the telegraph from Papa?

Emma broke into a run. The streets were muddy and her boot heels sank deep.

When she leaped onto the stoop, Mama asked, "Emma, what happened to your hat?"

"Nothing...I mean...the wind blew it into the river. Is that from Papa? What did he say?"

"Yes, dear," Mama said, smiling down at the telegraph. Her face glowed for the first time since they'd started the journey. "He eagerly awaits us. If all goes well, we will see him in three days."

Emma sang out a loud hurrah, startling the strollers on the street. The cigar almost fell from Doctor Burton's mouth.

"Emma," her mother scolded. "Young ladies do not make such public displays. Now we need to purchase a new hat for you. And Kathleen"—she gestured to the maid—"we need to find you a new dress. That one is strangely black and tattered and won't be suitable for the rest of the river journey."

Kathleen curtsied. "Thank ye, ma'am. Thank ye very much."

"Yes, Mama. Thank you." Emma tried to sound grateful, too, but her thoughts were on her father. As the four of them made their way to the general store, her heart continued to sing silent "hurrahs." In three days she'd be with Papa!

* * *

That evening the *Sally May* departed for Lexington. Emma headed to the main deck after supper, a bunch of carrots hidden under her pinafore. At the general store, she had begged her mother to buy them for Twist.

Mama had eyed her suspiciously. Emma had hastily told her that Mister Jenkins had promised to take them to the pony. The pockets of her pinafore held other treasures from the store: sardines wrapped in paper, a box of crackers, and a licorice twist. "Since when do you have a taste for sardines?" Mama had asked. "Always," Emma had assured her, not telling her that they were for an Irish lad she needed to thank.

If I can find him, she thought as she hurried past the stove on the main deck. She had no idea where Patrick might be. Working with the roustabouts? That meant he'd forsaken her pony. Guilt tugged at her as she imagined Twist, his tongue hanging with thirst. The carrots were an apology for forgetting him and spending the afternoon in Jefferson City. She loved her pony more than she loved anyone else except Mama and Papa. Not seeing to his care was unforgivable.

"Horses are dumb beasts," Cousin Minna had remarked the only time she'd gone to the stable with Emma.

Cousin Minna isn't always right, Emma decided. The sun was setting, lighting the shadowy main deck with a glow. Emma passed a family huddled in a cave they'd made of some crates. The father was breaking a hunk of cheese into pieces. Four grubby children stuffed the bits into their mouths. A baby, wrapped in a thin blanket, screamed in his mother's arms.

As the children chewed, they stared at Emma with hollow eyes. She had just finished a meal of roast turkey, rabbit stew, and apple pie. She ducked away, her insides twisting at the thought of this family's hunger.

At home in St. Louis, their servants had eaten well. After Papa left on his trip, Emma often sat in the kitchen with Mister Tommy and Cook eating scones thick with jam. Their laughter had made the house less lonely.

"Twist!" she called when she finally reached the animals. A neigh greeted her, and Emma's heart thumped with joy. She climbed to the top of the pen. Her pony gazed up at her. His thick forelock was brushed smooth; his star shone pure white. A full bucket of water stood in the corner. The stall floor was freshly bedded.

For a moment, Emma was too astonished to move. Who had cared for her pony? Had Captain Digby ordered one of the deckhands? Had Doctor Burton paid Mister Jenkins? Then she noticed the new sailor's knot tied in the rope. *Patrick?*

"'Tis about time ye showed up," Patrick said from behind her.

Startled, Emma lost her grip on the board and tumbled backward. She landed with a thump on the side of the milk cow, who mooed with annoyance.

Emma scrambled to her feet, tugging her skirt over her pantaloons. Manure stains dotted her pinafore and bits of straw stuck to her sleeves. "You should warn a lady when you approach," she scolded, flushing with embarrassment.

"A lady?" He laughed and leaned against the slats. A

porkpie cap that matched the red checks in his jacket was angled on his head, making him look older.

"What are you doing here?" she asked. "And where did you get that cap?"

"I bought it in Jefferson City with me pay."

"Pay?"

"Aye. First mate likes me mettle."

"And does he like it that you're a stowaway?"

He glared at her from under his brim. "Are ye aiming to tell him?"

Ignoring him, she reached for the top board. Patrick was up and into the stall before her. She hugged her pony, who snuffled her pinafore. "Here my sweet, I brought you a treat from the general store." She held out the carrots.

"Well? Are ye?" he demanded.

"I got something for you at the general store, too." She pulled the paper package and crackers from her pocket.

Patrick took them and settled in the corner to eat. "I gather that means ye won't tell him."

"I gather you're still caring for Twist?"

"A deal's a deal."

"Thank you. I'm glad we agree on something." While Emma brushed Twist's glossy coat, she watched the Irish boy eat. First he unwrapped the paper. Then he carefully laid three sardines across a cracker and stuffed it in his mouth. "You thought a fancy cap was more important than food?" she asked him.

He shrugged.

"In three days Mama and I meet my father," she went on. "Then we're traveling to California. Kathleen says you're traveling there, too."

Patrick stopped chewing. "You talked to me sister?"

This time Emma was the one to shrug.

"We have grand plans," Patrick said.

"Perhaps you could travel with us? I could ask Papa."

The boy frowned. "As yer servants?"

"Of course. Your sister is already planning to leave the employ of the steamboat. She could continue caring for—"

Jumping to his feet, Patrick tossed the paper and cracker box to the floor. "We don't need yer charity. Nor yer wages."

Emma sighed. This boy certainly was touchy. "Then how do you plan on paying for the long trip to California?"

"We'll manage without ye." Patrick jerked his thumb at Twist. "Look, miss, I'll continue caring for yer wee horse. But when we reach St. Joe, our deal is over and we'll part ways."

"You are so ungrateful, Patrick O'Brien," Emma said

as he climbed over the pen wall. "Perhaps I should have tattled on you to Captain Digby after all. Perhaps then you'd be more grateful for the offer."

Jumping to the ground, he turned and glared at her again through the slats. "And perhaps we should have let yer spoiled self burn up along with yer hat!"

"Spoiled?" Emma huffed. "For that you will not get your licorice!" she added, but he had already run off.

Fuming, she tackled Twist's tail with the brush. Perhaps it was just as well Patrick hadn't accepted her offer.

Her mother had grown to depend on Kathleen. The girl would have been great help on the journey west. But Patrick? He was a pigheaded boy who had neither proper manners nor clean clothes. Although...

Tipping her head, Emma thought for a moment. The first mate was right about one thing: Patrick *did* have mettle. Hadn't he shown his true worth during the fire? Hadn't he also kept his side of the deal even though she hadn't been very nice to him?

A gentleman always keeps his word, Papa often said. Patrick was more gutter rat than gentleman. However, Emma decided with a smile, her papa might just like him.

CHAPTER TEN

I ce is clogging the river," Mister LaBarge warned Captain Digby.

Emma peered out the front of the pilothouse, spotting the sharp, glistening chunks that floated on the river. The chill morning air blew through the open window, and she wrapped her scarf tighter around her neck.

"It might break the paddlewheels," Mister LaBarge continued. "And steering 'round the Lexington Bend is dangerous enough without ice."

"Aye." Captain Digby clenched his pipe stem firmly between his teeth. "We'll moor at Lexington until the sun melts the ice. After that, we'll waste no more time tackling that devil of a current. The passengers expect to reach St. Joe in two days. And by golly, I aim to have them there."

"Mama received a telegraph yesterday from Papa. He's riding south to Fort Osage," Emma told the men excitedly. "I hope this pesky river and its currents don't keep us from meeting him. He says he can't wait any longer to see Mama and me."

Captain Digby and Mister LaBarge exchanged glances. "And perhaps he'll be meeting someone else," Mister LaBarge said, winking at Emma.

Emma frowned. "No, no one else," she said. The two men started chuckling, and she wondered what was so humorous.

"Miss Emma, go below to help your mother prepare for landing," Captain Digby said abruptly. "And be quick." He was staring out the side window. Emma craned her neck to see why he was so eager to get rid of her.

Near shore, two towering black pipes jutted from the water. For a moment, Emma didn't realize what they were. Then she exclaimed, "Captain Digby, are those steamboat chimneys?"

"Aye. That's what's left of the *Martha Bee*. Now, get below."

Emma continued to stare, her eyes wide. A crow perched atop one of the chimneys was the only sign of life. "What happened?"

"It's best not spoken of, miss," Mister LaBarge said. "We don't want bad luck traveling the river."

"Bad luck? Did it sink?"

"Enough questions." Captain LaBarge shooed Emma away with his hand. "We'll be tied up in Lexington only a short while. I reckon your mother could use the fresh air."

"Yes sir." Emma rushed from the pilothouse, a brisk wind almost toppling her as she struggled across the hurricane deck. She held onto her new straw hat, glanced at the chimneys one last time, and shuddered. Perhaps Mister Jenkins would tell her the story of the *Martha Bee*.

Few strollers braved the morning, which was dark with billowing clouds. Missus Thornrose strolled with her poodle, and Emma gave them a wide berth. She wished she could take Twist out for air. Each day the main deck grew smellier and her pony more restless.

She had no idea what to expect when her family finally reached St. Joe. Papa had written of purchasing mules and a wagon. But these past two days, Mama could barely move from bed to washbasin. How was she to travel across the vast wilderness to California?

Perhaps Mama simply suffered with seasickness, and a night on land would cure her. Emma was tired of the steamboat, too. She was weary of the noisy paddle-wheels, the stifling staterooms, and the boring ladies. *The prairie is an ocean of grass and flowers,* Papa had written. A gallop across the prairie on Twist's back would be joyous.

Emma hurried down the stairs to the cabin deck. Mister Jenkins, who was bustling up the walkway, bumped into her. "Pardon me," he said, his gaze on the ledger in his hand.

"You are pardoned." Emma fell into step beside him. "I gather you are busy as we near Lexington?"

"That is true."

"Too busy to see the wreck of the *Martha Bee?*"

"It is bad luck to speak of wrecks." He lowered his voice. "And even worse to speak of the dead."

"There were many?"

"Indeed. Many immigrants, deckhands, and roustabouts perished. When a boiler explodes, those on the main deck rarely survive."

An explosion! Emma stopped in her tracks. She clutched her middle, thinking of Patrick and the families who traveled on the main deck. But she felt better when she remembered Captain Digby's reassuring words: *the* Sally May *is a floating fortress and Mister LaBarge its able commander.*

"I just came from below," Mister Jenkins went on. The man did like to talk. "The engineer discovered a broken section of paddlewheel. It needs to be repaired. Captain says we'll be docking in Lexington for the night. Will you help me pass on the word?" When Emma nodded, he strode off, pausing here and there to tell other passengers the news.

Emma found Mama and Kathleen in the ladies' parlor. Mama sat on a sofa, sipping tea and listening to Mrs. Hanover prattle on about nothing. Kathleen hovered nearby, her hands primly clasped together.

Emma skipped across the carpet. "We must pack a valise," she said dropping to her knees beside Mama's skirts. "We can stay the night in Lexington."

She told them Mister Jenkins's news. Immediately, Mrs. Hanover rose. "Dear me. We must hurry if we are to find accommodations."

"Go tell Doctor Burton," Mama told Emma as she struggled to stand. Kathleen darted over to help her. "Oh, a night sleeping on a feather bed on dry land," Mama said. "I have prayed for this."

"I'm sorry it will delay our reunion with Papa, though," Emma said.

Mama smiled. "Perhaps he will join us in Lexington. He is not far off."

"Perhaps." Emma thought excitedly of the possibility. "We must find a boarding stable for Twist, too. He is miserable below."

"Twist is an animal, Emma." Mama steadied herself on the back of a chair. "He will be fine onboard."

"No, Mama, he will not. And I will hold my breath until you agree he needs fresh air just as we do." Inhaling noisily, Emma squeezed her lips together and her cheeks puffed out like sails in the wind.

Mama raised her eyes to the heavens. "You will be the death of me, child." She sighed. "Find Doctor Burton and inform him that Twist is to be—"

"Thank you, Mama!" Before her mother could change her mind, Emma raced to the gentleman's cabin. As soon as Doctor Burton saw her coming, he slapped his cards face down on the table. "This time you will not give away my hand."

Emma rushed to tell him the news about landing. All the men at the table threw down their cards and rose, knocking over chairs in their haste. "Come." She tugged on Doctor Burton's sleeve. "Help me unload Twist."

"I will do no such thing."

"Then I will hold my breath until—"

"You may do so, child, until your eyes pop out and roll across the deck like marbles." He checked his watch. "Our responsibility is locating a comfortable room for your mother. However, I will see if Mister Jenkins can have Twist unloaded."

"Thank you, sir!"

Half an hour later, Emma stepped from the gang-plank onto the Lexington wharf. Steamboats lined the Missouri as far as she could see. Dark-skinned slaves, shouting peddlers, and busy deckhands surged around her. She trotted alongside the *Sally May,* searching for Twist. She glimpsed a flash of red. *Patrick?* She called his name, but the red disappeared behind a canvas sheet.

"Emma, stop that yelling!" Doctor Burton hollered over the noise. "I have given orders for the pony to be delivered." He was overseeing a roustabout who unloaded their bags from a handcart. Kathleen was helping Mama into a carriage.

"Delivered where?"

"To our destination. Now come before you fall into the river and we must fish you out like a carp."

Reluctantly, Emma left the *Sally May*. The doctor helped her into a waiting carriage, which was pulled by a handsome bay. The three ladies sat in the back seat, a fur robe draped over their laps. When the roustabout finished loading their baggage, Doctor Burton climbed up and sat beside the driver. "Where *is* our destination anyway?" Emma asked as the bay trotted from the wharf.

"Away from the incessant noise and smoke of the steamboats," Doctor Burton said over his shoulder. "Lexington is a prosperous town. My uncle owns several mercantile stores and a fine dwelling. We will be his guests for the night."

Emma rubbed the curly lap robe. "Mama, is this buffalo skin? Are we in the Wild West?"

Her mother only clutched the side of the carriage, wincing with each jostle of the wheels.

"That is lambskin, not buffalo," Doctor Burton said.

"But this *is* the West." Emma leaned her head over the side to get a better view. "Perhaps Daniel Boone is here."

"Daniel Boone has been dead for many years," Doctor Burton corrected. "Lexington is not some crude frontier town. It's a civilized city." He swept his arm in the air. "Here there are factories, churches, colleges, and a courthouse to rival the one in St. Louis."

"Oh." Disappointed, Emma slumped back onto the seat. The carriage rattled down a main street lined with stores, offices, and shops. Fashionable ladies with bustles strode along the sidewalks carrying their parasols.

Trailing along behind them were Negroes carrying baskets of goods, not Indians wielding hatchets.

The city is similar to St. Louis, Emma thought with a sigh. But then she perked up. Beyond the buildings, a wagon train wound up a hill like a snake. "Look, Mama. Wagons, like the kind Papa will buy for our journey."

"They probably belong to the trading firm of Russell, Majors, and Waddell," Doctor Burton explained. "The wagons carry goods to Oregon and California. My uncle trains and sells mules to pull them."

The carriage rumbled through the town and continued past fields, newly plowed and planted. The leaves on the trees were green with spring and wildflowers dotted the pastures. Emma breathed deeply. They'd only been on the *Sally May* for a week, but it felt like forever.

"Mama, will Papa find us way out here?" Emma asked, but Mama's eyes were closed and her head wobbled as if she were asleep. "Doctor Burton, will Twist find us way out here?"

"Enough with your questions. Be patient, child."

Leaning forward, Emma spoke to Kathleen, who sat on the other side of Mama. "Will Patrick be all right alone on the boat?"

Kathleen nodded, but her pursed lips told Emma she

wasn't offering any news about her brother. Finally the carriage stopped in front of a stately three-story brick home. Columns framed the marble steps, which rose to a wide carved door. A red-faced man with black mutton-chops covering most of his cheeks hurried down a brick path. Doctor Burton introduced Emma and her mother to Mister Phineas Burton, boasting that his uncle was one of the largest traders and slave owners in Missouri. Emma took in the man's barrel girth and decided that "largest" was a most appropriate description.

A slave unloaded their bags and then followed behind as they walked down the brick path. When they entered the hallway, they were greeted by two rows of curtsying and bowing Negroes.

"Mama, we don't believe in slavery, do we?" Emma whispered.

Mama placed a finger on her lips. "Hush, sweetheart. Thank you, Mister Burton, for inviting us into your lovely home," she said politely. "It is a welcome respite from the rigors of river travel."

"Please call me Phineas," he said. "Your husband is a good friend of mine, Missus Wright."

While they exchanged courtesies, Emma looked around. Her family's home in St. Louis had been modern and comfortable, but nothing as grand as Mister Phineas's house. The floor of the entryway was black and white marble. A crystal chandelier dangled over-head and a walnut staircase spiraled to the next floor.

"Is this a mansion, Mister Phineas?" Emma asked.

"Emma! Mind your manners," her mother scolded.

His eyes twinkled. "Yes, Miss Emma, it is the largest house in Lafayette County, designed by me and built brick by brick by my slaves." He gestured upstairs. "Missus Wright, you and your daughter will sleep in the guest rooms on the second floor. Annie will show you the way and tend to your needs." A young slave stepped forward and bobbed her head. "Your own servant girl can sleep in the quarters beyond the kitchen."

"Thank you, Mister Burton, but Kathleen will sleep with us," Mama said firmly.

Mister Phineas nodded. "As you wish."

Mama and Kathleen started up the stairs, but Emma snuck out the open front door. She wanted to be out-side and on the lookout for Twist. The sound of hooves rapping the dirt lane made her hurry down the steps. Trotting into view was a cart pulled by a swayback gray. A boy wearing a red jacket and cap sat in the cart bed. Tied behind the cart was a coal-black pony.

Twist and Patrick! With a squeal of joy, Emma dashed down the walkway to greet them, wildly waving her arms and shouting their names for all to hear.

CHAPTER ELEVEN

M ama sent me to bed with no supper," Emma told Patrick as the two brushed her pony the next morning. "Punishment for acting like a hooligan when I saw you and Twist."

They were in Mister Phineas's stable, a huge barn with peaked cupolas and stalls for four carriage horses and twelve fancy riding horses. "I call them my Missouri trotters," Mister Phineas had told her that morning. "Gaits as smooth as glass. They sell as fast as ice blocks in the summer."

"Sorry ye caught trouble," Patrick said. He was bent over, rubbing a dirty spot on Twist's hind leg.

"Oh, I didn't mind." Emma smiled. "I rather enjoyed being a hooligan."

Outside the stall door, a dozen slaves worked silently, raking the barn aisle. Last night, Twist had been placed in a large stall where he could stretch his legs. This morning, as soon as she awoke, Emma had led the pony outside so he could eat his fill of spring grass.

"And I didn't care about missing supper, either," Emma went on. "I was so glad to see Twist and...." She wanted to add *you* but she didn't dare. Emma knew it would not be proper. And besides, Patrick was already swellheaded.

"But no supper?" Patrick pulled a lint-speckled biscuit from his pocket. "Ye can share me breakfast."

"Thank you, but I ate this morning. We dined in a room the size of a concert hall, waited on by five Negroes. Mister Phineas made them stand at attention like soldiers. He'd snap his fingers when he wanted something. Can you imagine?"

Patrick gave her an odd look. "'Tis no different than being a servant."

"It *is* different," Emma argued. "Kathleen is paid a wage. And at home, Mama never snapped orders at our servants."

"Yer mother may not, but most do," Patrick said. "That's why Kathleen and me are going west to find our fortunes. One day we'll sleep in our own house instead of in a barn with the slaves as I did last night."

"Well, I'm going to ride," Emma said, tired of the conversation. She attached two ropes to the pony's halter rings. "Twist needs the exercise before we go back on the steamboat. Would you like to watch?"

"Ye have no bridle or saddle," Patrick pointed out.

"Twist is so well-mannered he doesn't need a bridle," Emma said. "And I often ride with no saddle." That was not completely true. Like the other girls in St. Louis from genteel families, she usually rode sidesaddle, a silly custom in her view. But a few times when no one was looking, Emma had straddled her pony bareback and ridden like a boy.

Opening the stall door, she led Twist outside. He trotted out happily, his ears pricked at the sights and his nose raised to the fresh breeze.

"My, you are glad to be off that boat," she said, patting his glossy neck. She glanced over her shoulder. Patrick was following several steps behind. Emma wondered if he'd ever ridden a horse.

They walked down a dirt lane bordered by a fence. On both sides, mules with big floppy ears grazed in the lush grass. Emma looked around for something to climb up on. She wasn't quite tall enough yet to mount on her own. Mister Tommy had always helped her.

She steered Twist beside the fence, climbed up two boards, and sprang onto the pony's back. Instantly she squeezed the heels of her boots into her pony's sides, and the two cantered down the lane. Her straw hat blew off, startling the mules. Twist gave a tiny buck, happy to be running in the open air.

Back in St. Louis, Mister Tommy had always made her trot in a ring. Sometimes he'd let her jump little fences. Always, he'd watched her with a cautious eye. Emma had never been allowed to canter free with the wind blowing through her hair and Twist's mane. Excitement filled her. She whooped, pretending she was escaping from a band of Indian warriors. What fun! She couldn't wait to ride across the prairie with Papa.

When they cantered back up the lane, she was grinning so wide her cheeks ached. "We outran those Apaches!" she exclaimed to Patrick, who sat on the top fence board staring at them. "Would you like to ride?" she asked.

"No." His expression turned sullen and he shook his head. "Me family were too poor to own a horse."

Emma slid off Twist. "Well, then, you need to learn how. You don't want to walk to California, do you? Perhaps Mister Phineas will lend you one of his fancy

Missouri trotters. Doctor Burton has already put in an order for two to be shipped to St. Joe for our trip west."

Patrick ran his fingers along his cap brim, then abruptly jumped off the fence. "All right. But don't be leading me like I'm a baby." Grabbing Twist's mane, he flung himself onto the pony's back.

Emma handed him the rope reins and stepped away. She had to bite her tongue to keep from telling him what to do. Twist had carried enough beginners to know he needed to walk steadily. Soon Patrick was steering the pony in circles.

"See? It's fun," Emma said. "Try a trot. Make a clicking noise and hold onto the mane."

"I don't need to hold on," Patrick retorted as Twist broke into a jog. Immediately he lost his balance and slipped sideways. "Whoa!" he hollered. The pony stopped and Patrick fell onto the ground like a sack of flour.

Emma pressed her fingers to her lips to hold back her laughter. She didn't want his pride as bruised as his backside.

He sprang to his feet. "Getting off needs a bit of work, maybe, but I believe I have the hang of riding."

Emma burst into giggles. "You do make me laugh,

Patrick O'Brien. When we reach St. Joe, you can practice some—"

"Miss Emma!" Kathleen waved from the door of the barn. "We just got word that the *Sally May* departs this noon. Hurry, we're loading the carriage."

"Tell Mama I'll be right there." She thought of Papa. There hadn't been time for him to meet them in Lexington. But soon she'd see him in Kansas City, which was only three more stops further up the river. Emma brightened. "Patrick, you must meet my father."

Patrick brushed off his pants. Then he straightened his cap and without replying, led Twist to the gate.

Emma walked beside him. "Wouldn't you like that?"

"I don't think yer da would want to meet an Irish lad like me," he said matter-of-factly.

Emma stopped. "Papa's not like that," she protested.

"Aye, he is, miss."

Her cheeks flamed. "You don't know my father, so don't judge him. I fear it's *you* who's too close-minded to meet *him*. Why, you're as stubborn as Mister Phineas's mules."

Patrick turned to face her in the stable doorway. Emma expected anger, but his eyes were sad. "Didn't going without supper learn ye what everyone else knows, Miss Emma? When we reach St. Joe, we'll be parting ways. Yer kind and mine don't mix. And for yer own sake, ye'd best be remembering that."

* * *

Emma stared grumpily over the railing into the river below. She was high on the hurricane deck, watching the roustabouts rolling barrels across the gangplank. Twist had been safely loaded and Mama and Kathleen were in the stateroom, but she had no idea where Patrick was.

Emma didn't want to think about Patrick. She knew he was right. Mama and Papa were civil and generous with their servants. But never had they befriended them. It was unheard of. Once they reached St. Joe, she would be safely in her Papa's arms while Patrick would be...?

She crinkled her brow, wondering what he and Kathleen *would* be doing. Perhaps they would end up staying on the *Sally May*. Patrick might get work as a deckhand, Kathleen as a chambermaid. Or maybe they'd work in St. Joe for a while as they'd planned, earning enough money to travel to California. Either way, Emma wouldn't see them again.

That was too bad. She enjoyed Patrick's company more than any of her friends from the St. Louis School for Girls. Frowning, she gnawed on her hat ribbon. What would Cousin Minna do?

Emma kicked the railing, knowing full well that Cousin Minna would never be in this dilemma. Her cousin would never have spoken to someone like Patrick, much less befriended him. Emma would have to come up with her own plan.

Resting her chin on her arm, she thought hard. *Of course!* She would convince Mama to hire Kathleen to care for her on their trip west. Kathleen was much more practical than her mulish brother. She would see it as a great opportunity. And if Kathleen chose to stay with her family, perhaps Patrick would travel with them, too. When they reached California, he could help Papa pan for gold. Emma could teach him how to ride like an Indian.

Mama was quite fond of Kathleen, Emma knew, so she wouldn't have to hold her breath long to get her way. But she did need to hurry. Captain Digby had announced that once the steamboat was underway, they would reach Kansas City by nightfall.

Emma raced downstairs. "Mama!" she called as she yanked open the stateroom door.

Doctor Burton stood at the foot of her mother's berth. Kathleen stood at his side holding a basin and rags.

Emma's gaze flew to her mother. She was propped on pillows. Her face was white and her eyes glistened. "Is something wrong?" Emma cried. Brushing past Doctor Burton, she knelt by the bedside and touched her mother's forehead. "Mama, are you ill?"

"You shouldn't be here, child." Doctor Burton had taken off his jacket and was rolling up his shirtsleeves. "Kathleen, escort Miss Emma from the room. Then bring me a pot of boiling water."

Kathleen set the basin on the floor and reached for Emma's elbow. "Come along, miss."

"No." Emma clutched her mother's hand. "Mama's sick, and I need to be with her."

Her mother forced a smile. "It's all right, Emma. I'm not ill. Go to the ladies' parlor. Missus Hanover is expecting you. Stay with them until we reach Kansas City."

"But I don't want to go with her and that silly Julia," Emma said. "What if you need me?"

Suddenly Doctor Burton's fingers tightened around her arm and he lifted her to her feet. "There is no time for arguments," he said. "Mind your mother." Roughly he propelled her toward the door that led to the main cabin. He opened it, gave her a push outside, and shut the door.

Emma whirled and pounded her fists on the closed door. This wasn't fair. Something was very wrong with Mama and she needed to be there!

CHAPTER TWELVE

The door opened, forcing Emma to step back. Kathleen slipped out, a finger held to her lips. She shut the door gently behind her. "Hush, Miss Emma," she whispered. "Yer only upsetting yer mum."

Emma choked back sobs. "Kathleen, you must tell me what's wrong. Is my mother dying?"

"Oh, no, miss. She's...she's..." Kathleen fidgeted, twisting her apron in her hands.

"She's *what?*"

"Soon you will have a new brother or sister."

A brother or sister? The shock dried Emma's tears. She stared at Kathleen.

"Now, miss, I've got to fetch hot water and help

Doctor Burton bring this child into the world."
Kathleen gave her a tired smile. "Don't worry yer head.
Babes are born every day. Now go and sit with the
Hanovers as yer mum wishes."

Kathleen bustled off. Still stunned, Emma stood outside the stateroom. *A baby?* Why had no one told her?
How had she not known?

Anger began to seep through her. She thought of
Papa waiting in Kansas City. What about their exciting
journey to California? They couldn't travel with an
infant. They would never reach the gold fields.

Papa's dreams—*her* dreams—would be ruined.
Disappointed and angry, Emma ran toward the stairs to
the main deck, wanting to be with Twist.

* * *

"Cousin Minna hates her little brothers," Emma grumbled to her pony a few minutes later. She was astride
him, leaning over with her cheek pressed against his
mane. "She calls them Rat and Worm. And Patrick
doesn't even know what happened to his father. I bet
the poor man fled on a long sea voyage to escape all
those noisy children."

Hugging her pony, Emma wallowed in her sorrow.

For months, she'd waited and prayed to see her father. The day was almost here, but there would be no joyful reunion. Emma pictured the immigrants' babies. They had mouths forever wide with crying and hunger. Mama would be burdened. Papa would be as disappointed as Emma was.

To make matters worse, she'd forgotten to ask her mother about hiring Kathleen. Now it was too late. The maid would not want to care for Mama *and* a demanding little baby. Emma would never see Patrick again.

When she'd run below to see Twist, she'd tried to find her friend. But Patrick wasn't among the shouting deckhands. And the roustabouts, who scurried to and fro with no thought of who was under their feet, had sent her fleeing to the animal pens.

"It's not fair, Twist," Emma continued to complain. "I never asked for a brother or sister."

She heaved a sigh, and the smell rising from the animals stung her throat and nostrils. After the fresh air of Lexington, the stench in the pens was unbearable. Twist reached around and snuffled her leg.

"I bet you miss being on the farm," she said to him. "And you'll miss Patrick, just as I will."

Spritzing noises from outside the pen caught her attention. Holding onto the pony's mane, she leaned close to the wall of the pen and peered between two boards, hoping to see Patrick. A woman was sitting on an overturned bucket, milking a cow. Beside her in the straw, a baby's round face peeked from a blue-fringed blanket.

Screwing up its brown eyes, the baby began to scream. The woman turned, dipped a finger in the milk, and stuck it in the child's mouth. For a moment it sucked hungrily, then again began to cry.

Emma frowned. *Will I never get away from babies?* She listened for sounds that the *Sally May* would be departing. Why was it taking so long?

Finally, above the infant's howling, she heard the hiss of rising steam and the *thunk thunk* of the paddlewheels. At last they were getting underway.

She slid off Twist's back. "Soon we'll be landing in Kansas City, and I'll be hugging Papa," she told the pony. "Perhaps I'll feel better then."

Giving Twist one last pat, she let herself out the pen door. As she made her way to the stairs, she kept her eye out for Patrick's red jacket. She spotted him on the starboard side of the stern, reeling in lines. She waved to him, but he turned away as if too busy to bother with her.

"Stubborn boy," Emma muttered as she headed upstairs. The cold wind had let up a little, and the boiler deck was filled with passengers. Emma loosened

118

the scarf around her neck as she climbed to the hurricane deck. Captain Digby stood between the two chimneys on the bow. He was hollering at the deckhands through the megaphone.

Emma hurried to the pilothouse. Standing on the steps, she poked her head inside. "Is everything full steam ahead for the *Sally May*?" she asked Mister LaBarge.

"Aye, Miss Emma. We'll need all she's got to make it 'round the Lexington Bend. The strong current and ice are still making it treacherous."

"Full speed!" Captain Digby shouted, as if he'd heard the pilot's words. "We'll crush this ice and beat this river or my name isn't Thomas Digby!"

Emma and the passengers cheered on the captain. All were eager to reach Kansas City. Mister LaBarge rang the bells, and Emma heard the roar of the boilers below. She peered over the wheel, trying to glimpse the "treacherous Lexington Bend," but saw only river and shore.

"Emma!" someone called. Doctor Burton was gesturing from the Texas stairs. "Your mother wishes to see you. You have a new sister."

Emma didn't move. *A sister.* A jarring thought hit her: What if Papa *wasn't* angry when he saw the new baby? What if he loved her sister more than he loved her?

"There is another surprise as well," the doctor added over his shoulder. "So come quickly."

"I don't wish for any more surprises," Emma said peevishly. But Doctor Burton had already gone. She scuffed her boot on the pilothouse steps, certainly not wishing to see that new sister.

Twist and I will just stay on the Sally May, Emma decided. She would work as a chambermaid like Kathleen. Or learn fancy knots and be a deckhand like Patrick. Later the three of them would travel together to California, pan for gold, and open a laundry. This new plan pleased Emma greatly. Saying good-bye to Mister LaBarge, she started below to make sure Mama was all right. She was curious about this new baby who was causing so many problems.

Emma headed for the stairs on the right side of the stern, nearest their stateroom. Suddenly a loud boom filled the air, and she was knocked to the deck. Her straw hat flew off. Cinders and splinters pelted her back.

Gasping, she flipped over and tried to figure out what was going on. Flames shot in the air. Roiling clouds of smoke hid the pilothouse and the Texas deck. She couldn't see Captain Digby or Mister LaBarge anywhere.

The *Sally May* had exploded, just like the *Martha Bee!*

CHAPTER THIRTEEN

Emma heard an ear-splitting shriek. One of the boat's chimneys appeared through the smoke like a ghost and fell toward her. Scrambling to her feet, she raced for the stairs. She took them in twos, tumbling down the last steps to the hurricane deck. The chimney hit the deck above her, rattling the entire steamboat. Planks snapped, and she scuttled like a crab behind a crate.

She covered her head with her arms. Cries came from all directions. Footsteps pounded past. Flames licked at the crate. *Mama. Twist. Patrick. Kathleen.* A jumble of names flew through her head. *I must find them!*

Peeking up, Emma searched for the stairs to the cabin deck. The steamboat groaned as if in pain and began to tilt. Was their boat sinking like the *Martha Bee*?

Fear and smoke choked her, but she could still see the stairs on the starboard side and the crush of passengers streaming down. Keeping low, she darted toward the stairway and clambered down to the cabin deck with the crowd.

There she froze while the rest of the people pushed past. What was left of the veranda railing stood in broken, jagged spikes. Cabin doors, which had been blown open, flapped like heavy wings. Billowing smoke filled the walkway in front of her and Mama's stateroom.

With another groan, the steamboat listed sharply, tossing Emma against the inside wall. Palms flat against the siding, she made her way in the direction of their stateroom. "Please keep Mama, Kathleen, and the baby safe," she prayed.

A man and woman rushed from a cabin, their faces spattered with blood. The man held the lady's elbow tight, guiding her. "Leave the boat, child, before it sinks," he said to Emma as they passed. "Save yourself. There is little left of the bow."

A sob welled in Emma's throat. *I can't leave*. Mama and the baby might be lying helpless in the berth. She had to find them.

Bending over, she coughed to clear the soot that

seared her lungs. Just then, another explosion rocked the steamboat. Emma grabbed a support post. A section of the veranda roof collapsed and splashed into the river.

Her heart hammered in her chest. "Courage," she told herself. Pressing her scarf against her mouth and nose, she plunged down the walkway and into the smoke. At the same instant a man burst from it and plowed into Emma. His hair was singed, his eyes bloodshot and wild. She fell backward, crashed through the broken railing, and hurtled downward. Landing with a smack in the river, she instantly went under.

Icy water closed around her like a black curtain. It pulled at her skirts and heavy boots and tightened the scarf around her neck. Emma ripped off the scarf, her arms and legs flailing. At last she reached the surface, gasping for air. A piece of flat wooden roofing banged into her. Ignoring the flash of pain, she grabbed the board and pulled herself onto it.

Shivers racked her body, but she swiped the water from her eyes and peered around. The current was spinning her downstream. She caught a glimpse of the *Sally May*—or at least what was left of the steamboat. The chimneys and the pilothouse were completely hidden in the smoke.

Emma remembered Mister Jenkins's tale of the *Martha Bee. When a boiler explodes,* he'd said, *those on the main deck rarely survive.* That meant Patrick, Twist, and all the crew and deck passengers were probably gone. What about Mama, Kathleen, the baby, and Doctor Burton? If only she had made it to the cabin. Could she have saved them?

Hot tears rolled down her cheeks. Dragging herself higher onto the board, she glanced toward the river-bank. Townspeople were streaming down the bluff and along the wharf. She tried to call to them, but no one could hear her.

She looked back to the water just in time to see a length of railing coming toward her, its splintered end as sharp as a lance. She kicked, trying to move her makeshift raft out of the way. But the rail rammed her left arm, ripping her dress sleeve and knocking her off the board. Emma struggled to keep hold of it, but the current pulled her under. She swam to the surface, gulping for air. Her left arm throbbed, and she could feel her strength ebbing.

She kicked and paddled, struggling to keep her head above water. Again she looked back at the wreckage. The *Sally May* was sinking, its stern stuck in the air like the tail of a duck bobbing for fish.

Mama, I'm so sorry, Emma whispered. She was exhausted and numb with the cold. Still she kept paddling, until at last she found another piece of wood to grab onto. Holding tightly, she let the current float her downriver for what seemed like forever.

Suddenly the water began to churn. Emma sputtered and raised her head. She heard a snort and a splash. A black animal appeared beside her. Its nostrils flared pink; its eyes were white-rimmed.

Twist! Grabbing the pony's long mane, she used her last burst of strength to drag herself onto his back.

The pony swam toward shore, his legs thrusting powerfully. Boxes, crates, and boards bobbled around them along with a pillow, a man's hat, and a lady's parasol. Then Emma spied a piece of red-checked cloth, puffed with air.

Patrick? She grabbed the jacket, felt the weight of a body. The current tried to suck the cloth from her fingers, but she held on. When Twist reached shallow water, he lunged forward. Emma fell off and found footing, her boots sinking into the muddy bottom. She tried to grasp the jacket collar with both hands. Her fingers were stiff and her left arm had no feeling, but somehow she managed to turn the body over. It *was* Patrick. Happiness brought tears to her eyes when she saw he was gasping a little.

Still clutching the collar, Emma dragged the boy

from the water. Exhausted, she collapsed onto the riverbank. Her soaked skirt weighed down on her legs like a sheet of lead. Her boots felt like sodden bricks.

Twist sloshed from the river onto the bank. Snuffling Emma's hair, the pony whickered anxiously. His mane dripped and his chest was covered with mud.

"Thank you," Emma whispered as she stroked the pony's muzzle. "Thank you for coming to my rescue." He still wore his halter and rope. "How did you get loose?" She examined the end of the rope. It wasn't frayed or torn. Had Patrick untied him? Had he made sure that Twist wasn't trapped when the boat sank?

She crawled across the gravelly beach to Patrick's side and placed her cheek by his mouth. A whisper of breath brushed her skin. Emma wept, thankful he was alive. He was cold, but she had nothing dry to cover him with.

Wiping her tears, she sat beside him. After the chill of the river, the afternoon sun felt warm. She looked upstream to the tiny speck of the *Sally May*. Several rowboats floated around the tip of the stern. Were they searching for survivors? A thimbleful of hope rose within her. Perhaps Mama and the others had made it after all. Emma remembered those spiteful thoughts she'd had about her mother and the new baby. How she wished she could take them back.

Beside her, Patrick moaned. Emma leaned over him. His eyes were closed, and his breathing was coming in wheezy gasps. When she felt his hands, they were icy cold.

She needed to find help right away. Twist stood behind her, munching a tuft of grass growing from the bank. She'd never be able to lift Patrick onto the pony. Riding for town would be the fastest way.

Emma forced herself onto wobbly legs. Holding onto Twist, she checked him for injuries. Finding none, she tried to mount. But when she raised her left arm, a wave of nausea set her head to spinning and she dropped back beside Patrick in a heap of soggy skirts. Gingerly she touched her arm. Her fingers came away sticky with blood.

"Emma!" A voice came from the river.

She looked up to see a man frantically rowing toward shore in a small boat. He was bearded, but she recognized the worried brown eyes. "Papa!"

"I can't believe I found you, child!" The hull of the skiff ground against the beach. Papa tossed the oars inside and scrambled out of the boat. Stooping, he gathered her to him. She buried her face in his jacket coat and cried with great noisy gulps. "Papa, you're here! But Mama, the baby, oh…I tried to reach the stateroom but I couldn't…and now they're gone and I didn't tell Mama how much I loved her."

He stroked her hair. "Mama and your little sister are fine."

"Fine?" Emma pulled back to search his face for lies. "How can that be? The *Sally May* exploded."

"I helped them escape. I arrived in Lexington about an hour before the *Sally May* left the dock. I made it onboard just as your sister was born."

"*You* were the other surprise Doctor Burton was talking about," Emma said.

Papa nodded. "Yes. When the first boiler exploded, Doctor Burton and I carried Mama from the cabin to the stern, which was slowly sinking. Kathleen took the baby. A fisherman nearby saw us and rowed us ashore in his boat."

"What about Captain Digby and Mister LaBarge?"

He shook his head. "I don't know, Emma. We will pray for the best. Now, let's get you to town. Your skin is like ice and you're trembling with cold." Taking off his jacket coat, he wrapped it around her. When the fabric touched her left arm, she winced.

"You've quite a gash, I see. And it is still bleeding." Hastily, he pulled a handkerchief from his pocket and wrapped her upper arm carefully. "That will do until I get you to a doctor. Come. I'll take you in the skiff."

"W-w-we can't go without Patrick and Twist," she said, her teeth beginning to chatter. "They s-saved my life."

"Patrick?

"Y-yes." Leaning over, Emma touched Patrick's hand. "He's...he's..." What? *An immigrant? Stable boy? Deckhand?* "He's my friend."

Papa knelt to inspect him. "He has a pretty good lump on his head, but his pulse is strong. The boat will hold only you and me. I'll come back for him and Twist or send someone. I promise."

"No, Papa. I won't leave without Patrick or my pony." Emma recognized Mama's steely tone in her own voice. "We can put him on Twist. I can use my good arm."

To show she meant it, Emma stood. Swaying, she picked up Twist's dangling rope and led the pony beside Patrick.

"All right then." Papa scooped up Patrick and draped him over Twist's back like saddlebags. "Can you lead the pony? That way I can walk alongside and keep your friend from falling."

Emma nodded. Gritting her teeth against the pain in her arm, she struggled up a path worn in the bluff. Twist walked slowly, one hoof in front of the other. Emma's feet slid in the sandy earth, and she almost toppled over. With her right hand, she held onto the pony's neck. Finally they reached the top.

There Emma halted, her eyes widening. A clover-sprinkled field stretched west from the riverbank. It was dotted with survivors from the *Sally May*. Some were sitting up, some lay quiet. Doctors with medical bags and townspeople moved from one injured person to the other.

Patrick groaned again. His eyelids fluttered. "Papa, he's coming to," Emma said. Just then, a man pushing a handcart spotted them and hurried over. He helped Papa lift Patrick from the pony and into the cart.

The man introduced himself as Mister Kerry. "The injured are being taken to the Lexington church where they've set up a hospital," he told them.

"Thank you, Mister Kerry." Papa bent so he was eye level with Emma. "Into the cart with you, too, daughter. I need to see about Mama. She's in Doctor Burton's care at a hotel. If she's feeling up to it, I'll bring her to the church to see you. She's out of her mind with worry."

"But first you'll take Twist to the livery?" Emma gave the pony one last hug. "He saved Patrick and me."

"I'll see that he gets proper care." Gently her father hoisted her into the cart next to Patrick.

Mister Kerry started off at a trot, and soon her father and Twist were far in the distance. Emma hated to leave them, but she knew Patrick needed a doctor. With each jostle of the cart, pain washed over her and chills wracked her body. Still she shrugged off her father's jacket and laid it over Patrick. "You're safe now," she told him, even though he hadn't opened his eyes and didn't seem to hear. And taking his icy hand in hers, she held on to him until they reached the church.

CHAPTER FOURTEEN

Emma huddled in the first pew, a dry shawl draped over her shoulders. Her damp, stocking-covered feet were warming on a heated rock. A muslin bandage was wound around her throbbing arm. A wood stove burned nearby, and she had finally stopped shivering.

Patrick was lying on the pew, his bare feet sticking out from the blanket someone had spread over him. Every once in a while he stirred and muttered something Emma couldn't understand, but he was still unconscious. A white bandage angled over his forehead, making him look like a pirate. His head rested on a Bible, and his red-checked coat was hanging on the end of the pew.

Moments ago, a doctor had checked on Patrick. "He's a strong lad. He just needs time to recover from the blow to his head," he told Emma. "For now it's best to keep him warm and quiet."

Behind her, the church door creaked open. Emma twisted to see if Mama and Papa had arrived. She longed to see her family. But it was another group of injured passengers arriving. The sounds of their suffering made her own wound seem trifling.

A woman lying on a blanket on the floor beside the stove moaned. "Water, please, water," she called in a heavy accent. Emma spied a bucket in the aisle. She slid off the pew and made her way to it.

She scooped a dipperful of water and knelt by the woman, who raised her head to drink. Her face was crusted with soot and burns. Emma was startled to see it was the immigrant woman who had been milking the cow just outside Twist's stall.

"My baby," the woman whispered after she'd taken several sips. She grasped Emma's wrist, spilling the rest of the water. "Where is she?"

"I-I don't know, ma'am," Emma said. "I'll fetch the doctor or someone who might know."

She found a man with a stethoscope dangling around his neck. "Sir, the woman by the stove—" But he waved her away as he hurried toward a person who had just been carried in on a litter. "I'll get to her when I can, miss."

Emma thanked him and walked slowly back toward the mother. She was sure Cousin Minna had never had to pass along such distressing news. Fortunately, the poor woman had fallen asleep.

Emma glanced around, wondering what else she could to do to help.

"Miss Emma? Is that you?" Patrick raised his head. His face was pale and streaked with mud.

"It is," she replied, relief washing over her as she went to him. "Are you feeling better?"

Touching the bandage, he grimaced. "Like an ox sat on me head. What happened?"

"The *Sally May* exploded. Do you remember?"

"I heard the first boiler blow, and the boat caught fire like a pile of tinder. Luckily, it started on the lar-board side. It gave me enough time to untie Twist and open his stall door before the second one blew." He shook his head. "I don't know what happened after that."

"The second blast must have blown you and Twist into the river," Emma said.

He propped himself up on one elbow. "But how did I get to shore? I can't swim."

"I saw you float by."

"Ye saved me?"

"Only after Twist saved me. If you hadn't untied him, the river would have taken us all."

His gaze shifted to the wounded people lying around

the room. "And me sister?" he asked, a catch in his voice.

"She's fine. My father came aboard at Lexington. He and Doctor Burton saved Mama, Kathleen and the baby."

Patrick arched his brows. "Baby?"

"I've a new sister."

"Emma!" Her mother's cry suddenly echoed through the entire church. She was holding onto Papa as they came up the aisle. Emma ran to meet them. She buried her face in Mama's cloak, her tears darkening the velvet.

"I prayed you would be safe," Mama murmured.

"Where are Kathleen and the baby?" Emma asked.

"They are outside in the carriage," Papa said. "Mama insisted that I bring her in to see you. She shouldn't be up walking around." He steered Mama to an empty pew, where she sank onto the wooden seat.

Taking off her shawl, Emma draped it over her mother's lap.

"I'm so happy to see you, my dearest," Mama said. "I couldn't bear it, thinking you might be...."

"I know, Mama." Emma swiped away a tear. "But we are all together now—you, me, and Papa."

"And Grace," said Papa.

"Grace?"

"Yes, my darling daughter. That is your new sister's name."

Grace was a nice name. *Perhaps it might not be all bad to have a sister,* Emma thought.

She looked back at Patrick. He was sitting up, the blanket around his shoulders. His hair poked up above the bandage, and without his cap, he seemed smaller. "Papa, Patrick would like very much to see his sister."

Patrick stood, one hand clutching the blanket around his shoulders. Stepping forward on shaky legs, he gave a polite nod to Emma's mother. Then he held out his other hand to Papa. "I am Patrick O'Brien, sir. I am pleased to meet the man who saved me sister."

"And I'm pleased to meet the boy who helped save my daughter," Papa said, adding, "Thank you." But Emma noticed that he didn't take Patrick's hand.

"I ain't no hero." Patrick tipped up his chin. "But I am a right steady worker. I watched over yer daughter's wee horse. And I helped the deckhands on the *Sally May*."

"Carrying four logs at a time," Emma chimed in. "And always making sure that Twist was properly fed and watered."

"So you're a hard worker with gumption." Smiling,

Papa took Patrick's hand and shook it. "No doubt the West can use men like you."

"No doubt," repeated Mama. "You'd be a fine addition to any venture."

"I thank ye, ma'am," Patrick said, flushing at the compliments.

"Papa, what news is there of Captain Digby and Mister LaBarge?" Emma asked.

"By some miracle, they both survived. They are working tirelessly, aiding passengers."

"Thank goodness they are all right," Emma said. "But what of the *Sally May*?"

Papa shook his head. "She is gone."

Emma frowned. "The captain swore the *Sally May* was a floating fortress."

"The captain and pilot are able river men, Emma." He gently touched her shoulder. "But the Missouri River has claimed many steamboats."

"I *would* be furious at that river," she said, wanting to stamp her stockinged foot. "Except it also brought you to us, Papa." Emma sat on the pew next to her mother. "Did our other friends make it off the *Sally May*? Mister Jenkins and Julia and Missus Hanover...?" Emma's voice grew thick when she thought of the crew and passengers that she'd gotten to know.

Mama tenderly touched Emma's hair. "We don't have news of everyone, sweetheart," she explained. "But the townspeople have been glorious in their rescue efforts."

"Now, no more questions," Papa said firmly. "Phineas Burton has graciously invited you, Mama, and the baby back to his house to rest. Twist has already been taken to his stable. Mister Burton's carriage awaits you outside. I need to join the rescuers. There is much to be done."

"I would like to help, too, sir," Patrick said, casting off the blanket. When Emma gave him a worried look, he quickly added, "Me head is fine."

"Good." Papa nodded. "Every strong and able person is needed."

"I want to help, too." Emma stood up to show she was as capable as Patrick.

"No, dearest," Mama said. "You are injured."

"Then let me stay and aid others in the church," Emma continued. "Or I will—" She stopped. She'd been about to say *hold my breath,* but she'd realized how foolish it would sound.

"I think that would be a wonderful way to give thanks for being alive," Mama said as Papa helped her to her feet. "Kathleen wishes to lend a hand, too. She can stay here with you. Grace and I can manage without you both for a little while."

"Come, Emma." Papa held his other elbow out to her. "It's time to meet your sister. Then you can come back to help."

She searched her father's face. "You aren't angry about the new baby?"

"Angry?" He raised his brows.

"Yes. Our trip to California will have to be delayed."

"Wagon trains will be leaving all of April," Papa said. "In a few weeks Mama and the baby should be ready to travel. But what about you, my brave daughter? Are you growing fainthearted at the thought of rattlesnakes, coyotes, and Indians?"

"Never," Emma said firmly.

"Good. Because I am counting on you and Twist to help guide us across the prairie."

"Patrick and his sister are going to California, too." Emma cast a sidelong glance at Patrick.

"Kathleen and I have already spoken," Mama said. "She says that traveling with us would suit everyone well. However, she said her brother must agree."

Patrick straightened quickly. "I do, ma'am! I've got gold fever the same as everyone else." Forgetting his injury, he retrieved his jacket and then rushed back.

Emma couldn't believe her ears. Everything had fallen into place, and she hadn't had to stomp her feet or hold her breath once.

"Good." Papa nodded. "Except I must warn you, I'm not headed to California to pan gold."

"You're not?" Emma exclaimed.

Papa laughed at her astonished expression. "No, child. The new state needs sharp businessmen as well as tough miners."

"Aye, sir!" Patrick chimed in. "I like the sound of that as well."

"We'll still have adventures?" Emma asked her father. "You, me, Mama *and* the baby?"

"A barrel full of adventures." Papa took Emma's hand and smiled down at her. "I promise." And she could tell by the softness in his eyes that he had more than enough love for both her and Grace.

"Though no more adventures quite as sad as this one, I hope," Mama said solemnly as Papa helped her down the aisle past the survivors.

When they reached the church doors, a man carrying a baby came in. Emma recognized the blue-fringed blanket. "Please, sir," she said. "This baby belongs to the woman by the stove. She has been asking for her."

Patrick held open the door for them, but Emma

paused to watch the man hurry toward the stove in the front of the pews. She heard the mother's cry at the sight of her baby, and her own heart felt full. The river journey had been filled with peril—yet there was some joy, too.

"I won't ever forget this trip on the *Sally May*," she said, her gaze meeting Patrick's.

"Aye, miss. Me neither."

"Come, Emma. You have your own baby to greet," Papa called from outside.

Emma quickened her pace and followed Mama and Papa to the carriage. Kathleen was walking back and forth beside the horses, cooing to the bundle in her arms. When she saw Patrick, she gave a cry of joy. He grinned, but ducked his head as if too embarrassed to throw his arms around his sister.

"Please, Kathleen, may I hold her?" Emma asked.

"Yes, miss." Kathleen placed the baby in Emma's arms.

Emma took the bundle gently. Then she pulled back the blanket covering the baby's face. Grace was puckered and pink, and when she opened her tiny eyes, Emma gazed with wonder at her new sister.

For once, she was speechless.

ALISON HART loves to write historical fiction because of the way history has shaped our lives today. She is the author of many books for young readers, including the three exciting titles of the Racing to Freedom Trilogy— GABRIEL'S HORSES, GABRIEL'S TRIUMPH, and GABRIEL'S JOURNEY—all Junior Library Guild Selections, and ANNA'S BLIZZARD, another exciting tale of a plucky young girl and her pony.

Hart lives in Virginia with her husband, two kids, three dogs, one cat, and two horses. She teaches English at Blue Ridge Community College in the Shenandoah Valley. Find out more about Alison at *www.alisonhartbooks.com*.

MORE ABOUT LIFE ON THE RIVER IN THE 1880s

EMMA'S RIVER: THE MIGHTY MISSOURI

TRADERS, TRAPPERS, AND GOLD SEEKERS used the Missouri River as a highway west. They traveled on rafts, on keelboats, and, beginning in 1819, on steamboats. Later, families like Emma's and immigrants like Patrick also used the Missouri River to travel westward. Soon the shores were dotted with towns, including St. Joseph and Lexington. They became jumping-off spots for people traveling to the California and Oregon territories.

keelboat

Between 1845 and 1860, steamboats also carried sugar, coffee, molasses, cotton, and hardware to western settlers. They brought back iron, lead, furs, hides, and pork products to the East. By 1890, steamboats had mostly disappeared from the Missouri River. They'd been replaced by trains, which were faster and cheaper.

river raft

THE REAL STEAMBOAT DISASTER AT LEXINGTON, MISSOURI

STEAMBOAT TRAVEL could be dangerous on the "Big Muddy." The Missouri River was full of logs, sandbars, reefs, rapids, and shallows. Fires, explosions, and sinkings were common. Between 1819 and 1897, more than 289 boats sank in its waters. Fog, high winds, ice, storms, and dark nights also made river travel dangerous.

wreck of the steamboat *Tennessee* on the Missouri River

In 1852, the real steamboat *Saluda* exploded. Like the *Sally May* in the story, it was leaving the town of Lexington, Missouri. Two-thirds of the steamboat blew apart. The captain and most of the crew were lost. More than seventy-five passengers were killed. Cargo and belongings were destroyed. James May, a traveler on the *Saluda*, wrote "all the little we had was lost." News of the explosion was telegraphed all over the United States. It was "considered one of the worst…steamboat disasters on the Missouri River."

THE BOILER DECK

DESPITE THE DANGER, steamboats were described as elegant "moving hotels." Cabin passengers like Emma traveled on the comfortable boiler deck. They were waited on by stewards, maids, and cabin boys. They ate three delicious meals a day and slept in their own rooms, called staterooms. They played cards and danced to music in the grand salon, the fancy main cabin.

Gentlemen were forbidden in the parlor, the ladies' part of the main cabin. Ladies could not enter the gentlemen's end, except for meals. The barbershop, baggage room, nursery, pantry, kitchen, clerk's office, and washrooms were also located on the boiler deck.

Belle Memphis—main cabin

THE MAIN DECK

BELOW THE FANCY BOILER DECK was the crowded main deck. This was where cargo, animals, crew, and immigrants like Patrick traveled together. Main deck passengers, called deckers, brought their own food and shared one stove. They dipped water to drink from the muddy river. Since there was no refrigeration, they brought bread and sausage, which would not spoil quickly. If a steamboat got stranded on a sandbar or iced in, the deckers often starved.

fur trader with pelt

riverboats at Memphis

One traveler described the main deck as "bleak and bare, no table, no utensils, a few dim lanterns, a long sheet iron stove, bunks on the side— reminds one of a horse stable." Deck passengers were not allowed on the boiler deck. Any decker who dared to go upstairs was immediately left on shore.

riverboat pilot in the wheelhouse

THE LIFE OF A RIVERMAN

STEAMBOATS needed many workers. Rousters, or roustabouts, moved barrels, trunks, bales, and wood to and from the steamboats. They carried their loads across narrow planks while the first mate yelled orders and hit them with a stick or cane if they didn't obey quickly enough. The work of the rousters was hazardous. They often slipped in the mud or tumbled off the planks into the river. The deckhands were the seamen of the steamboat. They ran out the boat lines and sounded for clear channels in the river.

Steamboats needed wood for fuel. "Wooding up" happened twice a day when the boats stopped at woodyards along the river. Rousters and deckhands carried four or five heavy logs onto the boat at a time. Workers called firemen then stoked the wood into the furnaces. The fire in the furnaces heated the water in the boat's boilers. The boiling water turned into the steam that ran the engines, which were manned by engineers. The engines then turned the paddlewheels that propelled the boat along the river.

passengers waiting to board the Falls City steamboat

Most rousters, deckhands, and firemen were rough-looking young men. Some were immigrants (mostly Irish, German, and Dutch). Others were slaves, free Negroes, or farm boys who wanted adventure on the river. Some workers slept in stacks of bunks in the cargo area. Others slept among the freight, animals, and immigrants. In cold weather, they covered themselves with straw, a sack, or an old coat to keep warm. They ate the food that was left over from the cabin passengers' meals.

The captain and the pilot were in charge of the steamboat. Captains, hoping to make more money, drove the overloaded boats fast and hard each trip. The pilot had the difficult job of navigating the windy, muddy river. He was called "the king of rivermen." He constantly communicated with the engineer using bells. As soon as he heard the signal, the engineer had to react quickly. His job demanded concentration and great skill. If there was trouble, the bells might signal "stop, back, slow, and full steam ahead" all at one time.

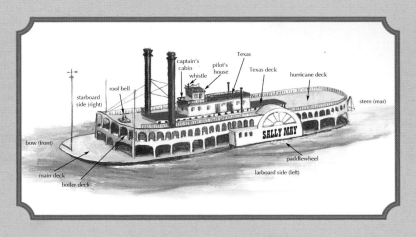

More about Life in the Mid-1800s...

ELECTRIC LIGHTS were not generally used until 1878. Emma and Mama had gas lanterns in their stateroom. Gas and lard or whale oil were used in lamps. The fancy chandeliers in the main cabin also used gas. Today, if you went camping, you might carry along a gas lantern.

Girls like Emma did not wear pants (called trousers or pantaloons). They wore skirts and dresses with long sleeves. A pinafore helped keep the dresses clean. Sometimes they wore frilly bloomers or pantalettes under their skirts. In December of 1852, a woman named Emma Snodgrass was arrested for wearing pants in Boston!

girl's traveling costume

In 1852, Missouri was a state. Kansas and Nebraska were still part of the area called the Nebraska Territory, which was considered Indian country.

Gold was discovered in California in 1848. This discovery spurred western migration. By 1852, many adventurous people like Emma's father traveled to California and Oregon. Some had gold fever, but others wanted to start businesses in the growing West.

AUTHOR'S NOTE

The quotes in the section called "The Real Steamboat Disaster at Lexington, Missouri" are from EXPLOSION OF THE STEAMBOAT SALUDA: A STORY OF DISASTER AND COMPASSION INVOLVING MORMON EMIGRANTS AND THE TOWN OF LEXINGTON, MISSOURI, IN APRIL 1852. The quote from the section "The Main Deck" is from STEAMBOAT ON THE WESTERN RIVER.

Special thanks to "Captain" Alan Bates for patiently answering my steamboat questions and for giving me a tour of the *Belle of Louisville,* the oldest operating steamboat in the United States and a National Historic Landmark. For more information go to *http://belleoflouisville.org.*

To Learn More about Steamboats

BOOKS:

Lang, Allyne H, Alexa L. Sandmann, and Renee C. Rebman. ROBERT FULTON'S STEAMBOAT. Capstone Press, Inc.: 2007.

Zimmermann, Karl. STEAMBOATS: THE STORY OF LAKERS, FERRIES, AND MAJESTIC PADDLE-WHEELERS. Boyds Mill Press: 2007.

WEBSITE: www.steamboats.org

The following books were invaluable in my research:

Bates, Alan L., and Adam I. Kane. THE WESTERN RIVER STEAMBOAT. Texas A&M University Press: 2004.

Beadle, Erastus F. HAM, EGGS AND CORN CAKES: A NEBRASKA TERRITORY DIARY. University of Nebraska Press: 2001.

Gillespie, Michael. WILD RIVER, WOODEN BOATS. Heritage Press, Wisconsin: 2000.

Hartley, William G. EXPLOSION OF THE STEAMBOAT SALUDA: A STORY OF DISASTER AND COMPASSION INVOLVING MORMON EMIGRANTS AND THE TOWN OF LEXINGTON, MISSOURI, IN APRIL 1852. Millennial Press: 2002.

Hunter, Louis C. STEAMBOATS ON THE WESTERN RIVERS. Dover Publications: 1994.

Sanford, Mollie Dorsey. THE JOURNAL OF MOLLIE DORSEY SANFORD IN NEBRASKA AND COLORADO TERRITORIES, 1857–1866. University of Nebraska Press: 2003.

Twain, Mark. LIFE ON THE MISSISSIPPI. Random House: 2007.

J
HAR

LCW

Hart, Alison,
1950-

Emma's river.

7.0